LAST CONFLICT

LAST CONFLICT

CLASSIC SCIENCE FICTION STORIES

JOHN RUSSELL FEARN

Edited by Philip Harbottle

THE BORGO PRESS

MMXII

LAST CONFLICT

FIRST EDITION

Published by Wildside Press LLC

www.wildsidebooks.com

DEDICATION

For David Ward

CONTENTS

ACKNOWLEDGMENTS

These stories were previously published individually as follows, and are reprinted by permission of the author's estate and his agent, Cosmos Literary Agency.

"Last Conflict" was first published in *Fantasy* #1, December 1946. Copyright © 1946 by John Russell Fearn; Copyright © 2012 by Philip Harbottle.

"Nemesis" was first published as "The Last Hours" in *Amazing Stories*, May 1942. Copyright © 1942 by John Russell Fearn; Copyright © 2012 by Philip Harbottle

"Three's a Crowd" was first published in *British Space Fiction Magazine* #13, 1955. Copyright © 1955 by John Russell Fearn; Copyright © 2012 by Philip Harbottle.

LAST CONFLICT

To the uninitiated youth from Paradise Acres, London was a monstrous giant that awed and overwhelmed him, yet which fired within him a reckless desire to master its hugeness. He stood at the corner surveying it all, an untidy boy of seventeen whose clothes bespoke the neediness of his upbringing. Passers-by glanced at him curiously, but did not speak.

He had heard that the city was divided into two great circles, the inner one containing all the wealth and brains it possessed, the outer relegated to the Workers, the humdrum wage earners with little ambition beyond their daily bread. The tremendous advance of science and social welfare had laid their impress upon this new London of the early part of the twenty-second century, but in the process of the change had come a sharp cleavage between its citizens. Now, one was either very rich or very poor, very intelligent or very dense, the sole key to power being either exceptional ability or wealth.

Young Melvin Read, at the street corner, had very little money. But he was more than assured of his abilities.

"Looking for something, sonny?" a voice asked at his elbow. He glanced up at the burly figure of a city police officer.

"Yes," he nodded, entirely confident. "I'm looking for the Scientific Institute. I have an appointment there."

"That's the Institute down there." The constable pointed, then looked at the boy doubtfully. "You know, by rights I ought to detain you at the station while your circumstances are looked into."

Melvin frowned. "I don't understand."

"Which shows you don't belong to this city. Everybody here, Intellectual or Worker, knows the regulations."

"I'm from Paradise Acres," Melvin explained. "I came here first thing this morning, by monobus."

The officer reflected, as though uncertain where his duty lay. Paradise Acres was a garden suburb beyond the outskirts of the city proper, a backwater of the Workers, despised by its neighbours.

"Well?" asked the boy, challengingly. "Are you going to run me in or not?"

"No—but I should. Better be on your way before I change my mind." The officer's eyes twinkled.

Melvin nodded, murmured his thanks, and hurried through the crowds of shoppers and strollers in the afternoon sunshine. He was grateful for the shade of the Institute's great hall, and paused for a moment to get his bearings, At length he saw the door of the reception office. He opened it quietly, closed it carefully behind him, and found himself in a deserted, well-furnished room with a fan whirring softly in the ornate| ceiling.

"State your business, please!"

He gave a start and cast a bewildered look round. On a screen set in the wall he saw the stern visage of a woman, and below the screen a loudspeaker.

"Name, please, and nature of business," the image insisted. "Speak plainly. The pick-ups will carry your voice."

Melvin cleared his throat. "I'm—I'm Melvin Read, from Paradise Acres. I've got an appointment with Mr. Colin Melbridge. He works here. He's a scientist."

"When was this appointment made?" the woman asked, acidly.

The boy hesitated before he replied. "Five years ago."

"Five years ago! Hmm—just as I thought! A cheap trick to try to gain admission to the Institute. Rebellious young men like you have tried it before, and I'm here to prevent it. For your information, Mr. Melbridge has been dead these two years as a result of a laboratory accident."

"Dead!" Melvin gasped. "But—but he can't be! I mean— Well, he told me to come here in five years' time and ask for him. I've witnesses to prove it—my brother Levison, and Lalia Melbridge. They were there when I asked Mr. Melbridge if I could get a job in the Institute, and he told me to come and see him when I was seventeen."

The woman's expression softened a little. "You mean

Miss Melbridge?"

"Yes, Mr. Melbridge's daughter. She was about thirteen then...."

The boy waited breathlessly as the receptionist considered. Then she said, tersely: "Your statement can be verified. Sit down, please."

The screen blanked and Melvin waited, anxious, but still hopeful. Presently an inner door opened and a slender, fair-haired girl in a white smock came in. He leapt to his feet, returning her stare. She hesitated a moment, then came forward with outstretched hand.

"Melvin Read! I couldn't believe it when they told me. I'm a student employee here. Do sit down."

She drew him on to a settee beside her, searched his serious, firm features with her clear blue eyes.

"I'm glad you remember me," he said, awkwardly. "I didn't get a very warm reception from the old battle axe—"

"Miss Hart?" She laughed. "Oh, don't take any notice of her! But you—you came to look for Dad?"

"I've heard about him being killed, from Miss Hart. I'm sorry—for you, I mean, not because he can't help me. But I'm still in earnest, Miss Melbridge. I love scientific things, and I want a job in this city. I'm only a Worker's son, but—"

"Call me Lalia," she encouraged. "Like you used to. You know, you really deserve a job here as reward for your patience and determination. I owe it to you, anyway, if I'm to keep Dad's promise. Just think how it all started when you and your brother saved me from drowning in that brook at Paradise Acres five years ago. I was trying to fish—remember?"

The boy nodded, his grey eyes reflective. "I've often wondered what your father must have thought of us and whether he remembered. He asked us what we wanted as a reward for saving you. Levison didn't want anything, and I asked for a job in the city when I grew up. Your father told me to come and see him in five years' time, and to study some special science until then. And I've done that, Lalia."

"You have? What subject?"

"Atomic physics, the same as Levison. He wants to be a scientist too, only he hasn't the ambition that I have. He's got some idea about helping other people with his knowledge, no matter what it costs him. Silly, really—he'll never get anywhere. I want to help myself, to make enough money to stand on my own feet like my father did. He was clever; he would have been an Intellectual by now if— Oh, Levison's a fool!" he finished, irritably.

Lalia looked puzzled. "Rather strange to find twins with such different temperaments, isn't it? You are twins, aren't you?"

He nodded, sullenly. "We're identical in looks, but in nothing else," he assured her. He was silent for a moment, then went on urgently; "I need a job, Lalia—badly. Science is the only thing that interests me, and I need money to help Mother at home. Levison's started to make a little money, but one of us has got to make lots of it, and I'm the one. I've studied hard these past five years, hoping your father would keep his promise to me. He isn't here now, but if you could help me—"

She pondered. "Dad was a senior Chemist, and I'm only a student at the moment, with no influence whatever. All I can do is put your case before the Chief, Mernas Steele, and see if he can let you sit for an examination for the Electronics Department. Dad was a great friend of his; he helped him in his early days. If I told him about Dad's promise—"

"You'd really do that?" The boy's eyes widened.

"You saved my life, didn't you? Come along with me," she said.

* * * * * * *

Lalia Melbridge had taken a big risk on behalf of Melvin Read and it was only later that he realized it. Had he not proved himself unusually promising when it came to the examination, the girl might have been discharged for allowing such a rank outsider to seek admission to the hallowed precincts of the city's Intellectual Circle. But as it happened Melvin more than justified himself, and his untiring application to the post that automatically followed soon established him firmly.

Indeed, though she had inherited much of her father's ability, Lalia found it hard to keep pace with Melvin's brilliance. He began in a fairly lowly position, and remained so for a year—then his uncommon skill earned him the position of overseer of a small student section. From then on there was no stopping him. Spurred by the streak of ruthless ambition in his nature, in five years he had become third in importance in his Department; and in ten years, though still but twenty-seven, he was answerable only to the Chief Scientist for his decisions.

To Lalia, watching his meteoric progress with quiet interest, he was a man to admire. His general brusqueness she dismissed as the natural manner of a busy, astute thinker, and she accepted his orders without question. Pride admiration, love—she experienced all these emotions in turn, and wondered if any feelings other than his passion for science and his driving ambition ever stirred beneath his hard exterior. Finally she set herself to find out.

Melvin found her at the door of his home one summer evening, almost ten years to the day since he had entered the city as an immature youth. He lived on his own in a special residential quarter of the Intellectuals on the rim of the city's inner circle, which was carefully separated from the outer ring of humble Workers' dwellings by a broad belt of green parkland segmented by great highways radiating like spokes from the towering central hub.

"Why, Lalia!" He was obviously surprised to see her at the door, her neat little runabout just outside the gate. "Come in—if you'll forgive the general untidiness. A bachelor home, you know...."

"You need a wife," she smiled, as he took her coat. But he seemed not to notice the remark and motioned her to his study across the hall.

"Make yourself at home," he invited, reaching for a silver box. "Cigarette?"

His grey eyes met hers over the flame of the lighter. She asked: "You don't mind my coming here? Your neighbours may question the ethics, since this is the house of the Vice-Chief of Electronics. It might start gossip, though I didn't think of it until I'd almost got here."

"Then it does no good to think of it now," he said briefly, as she sat down. "I'm sure you have a perfectly good reason for coming. As for the narrow minds and prattling tongues of my neighbours, one day they'll be proud of having lived within a mile of here."

Lalia only smiled. She was used to his egotism.

"I suppose," he went on, "you did come for some special reason?"

Her upturned gaze was steady as she replied, softly: "I came to see if you are the lonely man I think you are in private life."

"Lonely!" He gave her a keen look. "The busy man is never lonely, Lalia. I have plenty to occupy me."

She hesitated. "Don't you think I might share your interests—help you? I've a good scientific knowledge, have worked beside you for ten years. Doesn't it all count for something?"

He looked down at her pensively, then smiled tautly as he sat down beside her. "You sound like a woman in love!"

"All right, I am. You'd have seen that long ago if you hadn't been so wrapped up in your work. Not that

I blame you; you've done very well. But surely you can afford to relax now and again? There are other things—"

He shook his head impatiently. "I can't relax, Lalia, until I've achieved the objective I set myself as a boy—nothing less than absolute control of this city."

She was silent for a moment, her fair head bowed. Then, suddenly, she said: "You're aiming high, aren't you, trying to attain the Mastership? It will take you another twenty years. We won't be young any more then, Melvin."

"You believe in taking things into your own hands, don't you?" he remarked dryly. "Of course, I can see your point of view. Womanlike, you think our ten years of friendship and your help in the beginning give you the right to own me."

"Nothing so unpleasant," she objected quietly. "I am suggesting, since you seem too occupied to consider it yourself, that we get married. Why not? We have the same interests, the same ambitions, and you must know I would never have done so much for you if—if I hadn't loved you from the start."

"Marriage," he answered slowly, "is an emotional distraction I can't afford at this moment. With a beautiful woman like you for my wife, I might lose my grip on essentials. But—"

She sat waiting for him to continue. For a while he seemed to be weighing something in his mind. Finally, he nodded in decision.

"There's no point in attaining my objective entirely

alone. In fact, your help is just what I need at this stage. Let me show you something."

He moved to a wall safe and took out a roll of blueprints, laid them flat on his desk, and switched on the reading lamp so that the light fell across them. She rose and stood beside him.

"Something electronic?" she asked presently.

His grey eyes narrowed. "I believe this will give me the Mastership. The idea has absorbed my mind this past ten years. With this machine I can control the weather. Think what that means in a climate like ours."

"But that's wonderful!" Her admiring gaze was on him. "But," she added, dubiously, "Rufus Latimer will never give up the Mastership. He's too popular, anyway."

"Popular!" His tone was contemptuous. "Popularity isn't power. He may have earned his position by his contribution to science, but he can't keep it forever and he's had it long enough. I have here something greater than Latimer ever conceived. Once the Intellectuals know of it—and they will, very soon—they will have to depose him in my favour. If they don't—"

She almost recoiled from the glare he gave her, the fierce determination in his voice. He saw her startled look, recovered himself quickly, and said in even tones: "Produce something better than the Master and you become the Master. That's the rule, isn't it?"

Suddenly he seized her hands in his own, looked into her face in desperate earnest. "Listen, Lalia. Wouldn't it be better to build this machine before we turn to more personal matters. It's a great bargaining weapon, and Master and Mistress of London is better than plain Mr. and Mrs. Read, isn't it?"

She was smiling now. "Perhaps," she said. "Though I haven't got your all-consuming ambition, remember. Still, if you want it that way—"

"Good!" His smile was broader than she had seen it for many years. "You've solved something of a problem for me. I'd been wondering how I was going to get this machine built quickly and secretly, without assistance. I want the help of someone I can trust. If we work together at the Institute at night, we can finish the machine in three months. Nobody can question what we're doing if I have authorised it—except Steele, of course, and I can satisfy him all right. And it really needs two people to construct a machine as intricate as this one."

"How does it work?" she asked, frowning over the blueprints.

"Quite simply, it will produce reactions in the atmospheric layers and vary the pressures normally controlled by wind action, thereby achieving climatic stability."

The girl's frown deepened. "You're not too generous with the details, are you?" she said. "In these plans—" She stopped, and her brows lifted slightly. "But perhaps you don't want to tell me too much about it?"

He regarded her steadily as he rolled up the prints.

"I ask you to co-operate with me, Lalia, without my having to explain more than is necessary for your part in the actual construction. It isn't that I don't trust you, but what you don't know you cannot repeat, even in an unguarded moment."

She sighed and gave a little shrug.

"You're a queer fellow, Melvin. But geniuses usually are, of course, so I must make allowances."

She turned away from the table, and for a fleeting moment the frown returned as a faint, half-formed suspicion crossed her mind. But she banished the thought as quickly as it came, turned to face him again.

"When do we start?" she asked.

* * * * * * *

The building of the Elements Controller was a slow and arduous task for Lalia and Melvin, since the time they spent on it was always dependent on their freedom from official duties. But gradually, by unremitting devotion to their labours, they progressed.

The girl found her own part in the work limited to the assembly of various electronic components with which she was familiar, though their functions in Melvin's complicated apparatus she comprehended but dimly. The more intricate construction Melvin insisted on doing himself, usually when she was unable to be present. Noticing this, and his continued reluctance to discuss any but the most innocuous details with her, she more than once found herself considering if the Elements Controller was all it seemed to be, from what she had been able to grasp of its underlying principles. But each time she dismissed the suspicion as imaginary.

The summer passed as they went on working in a deserted wing of the great Institute, where Melvin had seen to it that no curious technician could pry without his knowledge, and they could proceed without interference or interruption. Autumn came, and winter, and still they worked almost every night under the shadowless glare of cold-light globes.

More and more, as they made headway, Melvin was consumed by an obvious impatience for the day when the machine would be complete. By the spring they had begun the final assembly of its several parts, and with the return of summer it was built—a great, glittering mass of crystalline bars, vacuum tubes, transformers, and radial fans. In all it covered a hundred square feet of floor space and stood eight feet high, connected by numbered cables to a master switchboard.

"Finished at last!" Melvin breathed, as he completed his final inspection of its more delicate intricacies. "The hand that operates that switchboard will wield power greater than any amount of money can give. What do you say, Lalia?"

The girl appraised the massive machine critically as she stood aside, hands thrust in the pockets of her work-worn smock.

"You speak of power," she said. "I've noticed, though, that you don't seem to have made any provision for power with which to run this machine. You have meters on the switchboard going up to millions of volts, yet I see no sign of any contacts for power cables.

Odd, isn't it? Or is the question out of order?"

Melvin smiled patronisingly. "I have taken that into account, believe me. I shall produce all the power I need myself, by a special process. When I make the first test tomorrow, you will see for yourself. Naturally, I don't want to excite suspicion by putting a sudden load on the city's power resources."

He paused, glanced at the electric clock. "There's time enough to have a little celebration over at my place, if you'd care?"

* * * * * * *

Twenty minutes later they were settling down to a meal produced by the kitchen automat, when the doorbell buzzed. Melvin got up, and went out into the hall. Lalia waited expectantly, heard the sound of voices that were curiously similar; then Melvin came back into the room followed by a man who was the exact double of himself—except that he was smiling.

"Lalia, this is my brother Levison. You've met before, of course, but it's a long way back."

"So this is Lalia the woman!" Levison took her hand warmly. "Just as beautiful as I'd imagined from Melvin's letters. Well, I am glad to see you—it's been a long time."

"And I, too," she responded. "We've often talked about you, but you never seem to come to the city."

"Too much to do elsewhere. Besides, city life doesn't attract me—" He broke off. "I hope I haven't interrupted a little *tête-à-tête*?"

"As a matter of fact, you have," Melvin told him, "but you must stay and have supper with us and tell us what you've been doing."

"That's just what I came to see you about, Melvin," said Levison, as he sat down. "I felt I couldn't put it off any longer—I've been itching to tell you all along. You see, Lalia, I've lived out at Paradise Acres alone since Mother died, and I've nobody to talk to when I've something big to say."

"Well, we're listening," Melvin encouraged. "What's happened?"

"To put it briefly, I've found a way to amplify thought."

Melvin stared at him fixedly for a moment. "You've—what?"

"Thought I'd surprise you," Levison laughed. "I've done a lot of experimenting in the past few years, but it never amounted to much until now. So far, I've only got the idea worked out, but I know I'm on the right track. It goes deep into the science of vibrations—the sort of stuff you love, Melvin."

Melvin nodded slowly, a blank look on his face. His meal lay neglected before him. Levison went on talking in between his eating.

"I don't have to tell you that the brain gives off minute vibrations. The Harvard Institute of Science found that out long ago and even measured the length of a thought wave, which is about the same as ultra-short radio waves. Of recent years the British Telepathy Association have substantiated the fact, and have proved that these tiny vibrations can pass from brain to brain, if there exists what might be called a telepathic sympathy between them. The brain can both transmit and receive these minute impulses, but they are so weak that they are undetectable except in cases of deliberate telepathic transmission under the right conditions. For that reason we use speech or actions to convey our thoughts. The centre of thought remains sealed—nobody can really tell what another person is thinking."

"You mean you've broken the seal—made it possible for thoughts to be read?" Melvin asked eagerly.

"No, not that," Levison replied gravely. "I might be able to do even that, but personal thoughts were never intended to become public property. That kind of probing might wreck civilization—"

"But, man, think of the power it would give anyone possessing such a secret! Power to read the minds of rulers, to divine your enemy's plans—" Melvin was passionately interested, now.

Levison sighed heavily. "Same old Melvin! If you conquered the universe, you still wouldn't be satisfied. This craving for power runs deep in your blood, doesn't it? If you don't—" He glanced at Lalia, checked himself. "But to get back to my invention.

"I set myself to find a way to amplify thought, to devise a machine capable of intensifying the normal thought impulses of the brain a hundred, a thousand, ten thousand times if need be These amplified thoughts, if properly directed, might then overwhelm and influence the minds of every living being within an area, depending only on the amount of power used."

"A kind of mass hypnosis?" Lalia suggested.

"You might call it that, but what I have in mind is rather different. The actual amplifying of thought does not present much difficulty, since it is identical with the principle of the amplification of radio impulses. The trouble was to find a way of intercepting and directing thought waves, which emanate from the brain in concentric circles of gradually diminishing intensity, like the ripples from a stone thrown into a pond.

"The solution lies in an insulated helmet—and an insulator of the short waves of thought took some finding. But I managed it; and this helmet will prevent the thought waves radiating away in circles. Instead, they are trapped and directed by an electro-magnetic beam in front of the helmet. This beam strikes directly on a magnetic plate, which in turn absorbs the vibrations and passes them on through a step-up transformer into the amplifier, whence they are radiated from the transmitting antenna with vastly increased power.

"Of course," he elaborated, "what I call the helmet is actually a big inverted dome and will be a permanent fixture of the apparatus. The operator will sit underneath it with the brain area of the head inside it. You understand?"

Melvin nodded, his brow lined with deep furrows, grey eyes fixed immovably on his brother's flushed face. Then, as though with an effort, he resumed his eating while Lalia watched him curiously. Suddenly he put the inevitable question:

"And what do you propose to do with this machine? You said you had some special use for it in mind."

Levison was silent for a moment. When he answered it was in a quiet, serious tone.

"I am going to try to destroy all the evil, disease, and disharmony in the world."

With a start Melvin straightened up, laid down his knife and fork. His twisted features, as he stared at his brother, reflected a mixture of surprise, impatience, and utter incredulity.

"But—but what a fantastic idea! Do you really mean what you're saying?"

"I do," Levison assured him without looking up.

"But such a thing isn't reasonable!" Melvin protested heatedly. "I don't doubt your ability to build this machine and use it to amplify thought as you say you can. But the object! Why get such sanctimonious ideas, when you have it in your power to control the world if you go about it in the right way? You could force millions of people to do as you wished! You've a glorious chance to attain a position of supreme power!"

Levison sat back in his chair and calmly returned his brother's glare.

"I am only too aware of the vast potentialities for good or evil that lie in such an instrument," he said deliberately. "And I hope I have a full sense of the responsibility it places in me to ensure that it is used only for good. I intend to work according to the scientific thesis that good or evil, illness or health, beauty or ugliness, are all conditions of thought as expressed through ourselves. Remember how Jeans put it long ago, in his *Mysterious Universe*? 'All that we see are thoughts expressed. The rest is remote inference'."

With a gesture of annoyance, Melvin rose abruptly from the table. Ignoring Lalia's appealing look, he rapped out:

"Yes, yes, I grant you all that. But you could bend men to your will—for good, if you like. Think of the good you could do once you'd established yourself as top dog. Why, you could hold the world in the hollow of your hand!"

Levison laughed. "But I don't want the world. Only the chance to make things a little better. No man can hope to do more than that. Dictatorship brings its own downfall, and I'd do more harm than good that way."

"You two certainly are very different in your outlook," said Lalia, rising. "But you mustn't quarrel about it. Personally, I can see something in both points of view."

She took Melvin's hand in hers, drew him towards a soft settee, beckoned his brother to sit down beside her.

"Sorry," Levison apologised, "but I must go—lots of work still to do. I really came along to ask Mel to come over and see my designs for the apparatus. He may have some ideas for further improvements or spot some flaw I've overlooked. If you could come too, Lalia, I'm sure you'd be interested. How about tomorrow night?"

"I'd like to come very much. How about you, Mel?"

He seemed too immersed in his own thoughts to

reply for several seconds. Finally he nodded. "All right, Levison. We'll be along about eight."

"Good! Well, until tomorrow, then."

The girl took it upon herself to see him to the door. On the step he paused, turned to look down into her bright blue eyes.

"Tell me, Lalia, how do you two get along?"

She hesitated, averted her gaze for a moment, considering. "He's a little difficult at times," she admitted, a faint smile trembling on her lips. "If only he wasn't quite so ambitious...."

"I think he's already got as much as any man deserves," he said gently. "I'm sure he'll find that out, in time."

She watched him go on his way, closed the door slowly, and turned to see Melvin standing in the doorway of the dining room, a cynical smirk on his face.

"What a pity," he observed, "that such a brilliant mind should have such a strange kink."

* * * * * * *

The normal routine of the following day was so heavy for Melvin and Lalia that they had no opportunity to make a test of the Elements Controller. In the evening they drove out to Paradise Acres, where Melvin drew the car up at the gate of a little bungalow surrounded by trim flowerbeds.

Here on the verge of the unspoiled countryside, away from the endless throb of the city's heart, Lalia found an atmosphere of quiet contentment such as she scarcely knew existed, it was so long since she had been able to relax in such a setting. Though he tried not to reveal it, even Melvin seemed to find in the comfortable home an air of peace and well-being which to Levison was obviously the ideal state of existence.

After supper he led them out to a small but well-equipped workshop at the rear of the bungalow, where they inspected several pieces of apparatus in various stages of assembly, the purpose of which he explained to them. Melvin listened attentively, asking questions only when he seemed not to grasp some particular point he wanted to absorb, and then very cautiously, almost apologetically.

At length, finding it difficult to convey an exact impression, Levison went to a drawer, took out a sheaf of small diagrams and spread them out on a workbench.

"Here, look them over carefully and see what you think of them. They explain the whole process from start to finish."

Melvin glanced at his brother strangely before he moved to the bench. He stood there for a moment, his back to the drawings, before he asked:

"Are you sure, Levison, that you're not being too trusting with your secrets? I want to help you, of course, but—"

Levison smiled, glanced through the skylight at the darkening summer sky, and switched on the light above the bench, flooding it with brilliance.

"What kind of man would I be if I couldn't trust

my own brother?" he countered, quietly. Then, leaving Melvin to his inspection, he turned to occupy Lalia with further discussion of his experiments.

For some time Melvin pored over the drawings, examining each in turn. Finally he fixed his attention on one of them, and stood motionless above it for a full minute before he straightened up.

"Looks all right to me, Levison," he announced. "I can't see any reason why it shouldn't work out, though you can't tell for certain until you've made a more comprehensive test than you've been able to do so far. You say your experiments to date have confirmed all your theories?"

"Absolutely," Levison declared, gathering up the drawings and returning them to the drawer. "As I was saying last night, I believe that thought rather than mere matter is the true basis of our universe; that matter is the medium through which thought expresses itself. In the case of human beings and other organisms which we call living entities, the body is the medium. Whatever our mind wills, the body must obey; and disease and all evil conditions and motives, if not the expression of our own thoughts, are due to the influence of other thought vibrations more powerful than ours, which are always present. I believe that my Amplifier, by enlarging the power of thoughts which will produce only the best possible conditions, will overcome those which result in undesirable states of being and exert a considerable influence for good."

There was the slightest suggestion of a sneer in

Melvin's smile. "And if the operator willed otherwise?"

Levison waved the question impatiently aside as though it was not worthy of consideration.

"It will be some time before I complete the apparatus," he observed. "But I've made quite good progress in the last few months. Of course, I'll let you know how things turn out. Shall we go back into the house now? I'm sure Lalia's had enough of this."

They sat and talked of other things, recalling their childhood days as they relaxed once more in the bungalow. Lalia had expected Melvin to tell his brother of his own work on the Elements Controller which had been his ruling passion for so long, but he did not so much as hint at it. She marvelled at the contrasting characters of these twin brothers, one so ingenuously frank with his inmost thoughts, the other so cautious and secretive. But she found herself excusing Melvin his reticence on the score of his natural affection for his brother despite his lack of sympathy with Levinson's idealism. Perhaps he did not want to overshadow his yet uncertain researches with his own accomplishments.

At the same time she seemed to sense in Melvin's attitude towards his brother something which suggested an infinite respect for his attainments, and something almost of envy, as though what he had already achieved was worth more than the finished, if untested, product of his own devising. Though his assessment of its value was very different from Levison's.

He was silent as they drove homeward, gazing steadfastly ahead through the windscreen at the myriad lights of London spread out before them like an array of jewels. Full of her thoughts, Lalia lay back in her seat beside Melvin and did not attempt to draw him out. Not until they were engulfed in the city's effulgence, its floodlit buildings rearing up on either side of them, did he reveal his feelings. They were much as she suspected.

"Brother Levison seems to have something in that Thought Amplifier of his. If only he weren't such a fool as to think he can reform the world by gentle persuasion! What it wants is force. Think what a power such an instrument would be in the hands of one man—one master!"

"You, for instance?" She could not resist the sally.

He shot a quick glance at her but did not reply. He said no more until he took his leave of her when they drew up at her flat in the centre of the city, and then it was only a perfunctory, "Goodnight. See you tomorrow." Almost before she had closed the car door he was on his way again.

As soon as he arrived at his own home he went down to his private laboratory in the basement, and removed the jewelled collar-pin he had been wearing all the evening. Switching on a red lamp, he laid the pin carefully down on a bench, produced a delicate instrument from his pocket, and with it unscrewed the massive diamond from its gold setting. It was evident now that this was no ordinary jewel, or even an ordinary imitation. The centremost, biggest facet was, in fact, a finely graded minimising lens with a minute iris-diaphragm behind it, actuated by the pressure of light-wave photons. The flood of radiance above the bench in Levison's workshop, when he had turned towards it, had been just what he required to make the shutter open and close two hundred times faster than a blinking eyelid. And his brother had switched it on for him, leaving him only to take up a position that would ensure a correct focussing of the tiny camera upon the drawings spread out on the bench. Just in case there were a few details he could not memorize exactly....

Smiling to himself, he fished inside the hollow setting of the jewel with his slender tweezers, extracting a microscopic strip of film. To develop and enlarge the image was the work of a few minutes. Switching on the normal lighting, he examined the perfect copy of Levison's designs that it presented.

"Yes, my misguided brother," he mused, aloud. "You can trust me—to see that your patient efforts are not wasted as you would waste them. If you don't want the world, I can use it!"

* * * * * * *

It was another three days before Melvin found himself free to undertake the first test of the Elements Controller. At seven o'clock, answering his call over the visiphone, Lalia presented herself in his office. She found him in the act of donning a heavily-proofed suit equipped with a dark-goggled helmet and lead-soled boots. She regarded him quizzically.

"Heavens, Mel! What's all this for?"

"Simply taking precautions," he told her. "It's likely there may be some pretty powerful radiations from that machine, and I want to be sure I don't get hurt until I know for certain what they are. They may be quite harmless, but—"

"Radiation? But why should there be? I don't understand. You've never mentioned anything of the sort before."

"We're playing with elemental forces, Lalia, and no precaution can be too great. But there's no need to fuss; everything will be all right. I just don't want to leave anything to chance, that's all. Since I haven't got another suit like this, you won't be able to come in the lab with me, but you can watch through the reinforced glass panel in the door."

She shrugged her slim shoulders, followed him along the corridor to the laboratory. He unlocked the door and went inside. She heard the click of the lock and stood watching him through the thick glass. She saw him fasten the helmet over his head, draw on the huge gloves. Then he crossed to the switchboard, threw in the master switch.

The dynamos began to hum, stepping up swiftly to a steady, high-pitched whine. From her position outside the door Lalia could not see the meter readings, but the delicate needles were visible, jumping along their graduated scales. There was power there—vast power such as she had never expected; and soon she saw the manifestation of it as the normal lighting of the laboratory began to dim before the flashing lightning of the machine's own creation. From the two anode and cathode globes at either end darted livid membranes of high-voltage electricity. Then, as the power mounted still further, they became violet-tinted chains leaping from globe to globe with crackling impact.

Lalia stood awed by the sight while Melvin, looking like some grotesque demon, worked over the switchboard, adjusting potentiometers and studying dials. Gradually, out of this wild chaos of unleashed forces was born a pale, lavender beam which rose from the centre of the machine, growing in strength and colour until it appeared like a massive amethyst column supporting the roof. Amid the flashes of his surging power. Melvin stood watching it, supreme exultancy in his attitude; while the girl could only stare, shielding her eyes against the incessant bursts of glaring light which gushed from the potential globes.

Minutes passed with that strange, transparent beam stabbing upwards to the roof of the laboratory, which, she assured herself, formed not the slightest barrier to its matter-penetrating substance. Though how high it reached she could only wonder, until a sudden draught from the ventilator shafts came sweeping along the polished corridor, bringing her to the realization that other things were happening outside. The big windows close to where she stood had lost their summer evening brightness and become dark rectangles of gloomy grey. With every second the external scene was changing.

Then, turning back to the glass panel, she caught

her breath as she saw Melvin straighten up from the switchboard, pass a gloved hand slowly across his dark goggles, stagger slightly, and fall headlong to the floor.

"Melvin!" she screamed, beating frantically on the door with her fists, though she knew there was little chance of his hearing her even if he were conscious. He lay there unmoving while she watched in growing panic. He had locked the door behind him. Had he thought this might happen? But to deny himself her aid— She could only stand there, bewildered, trying desperately to think.

Startlingly, from outside came a vivid flash of lightning that lit up the corridor, followed almost immediately by the violent crash of thunder. The draught was sweeping along the passage now in chilly gusts. There were splashes of rain on the windows—

In sudden decision she swung round raced down the corridor to Melvin's office. She paused in the doorway for a moment as a terrific flash of lightning dazzled her. Then she dived for the desk, whipped up a heavy paperweight and dashed back to the laboratory.

One—twice—three times she struck at the glass panel before it went sharding inwards. Hot, foul air wafted full in her face and set her coughing for a moment; then she thrust her arm through the opening, reached down until she could just touch, and turn, the key. As the door opened she hesitated, appalled at the crackling electrical hell before her. But the greater fear of what would happen if the machine was not stopped and Melvin rescued drove her forward, straight towards the master switch.

She seized the massive handle, tore the great blades out of contact. Instantly the lavender column vanished, the livid lightning from the great globes ceased, meter needles flicked back to zero. Sickened with the smell of ozone, her head swimming in the stifling heat, she grasped the belt round Melvin's waist with both her hands and dragged him across the floor towards the door. The cool air sweeping along the corridor soon revived her, gave her added strength. Struggling with the dead weight of Melvin's limp form, she managed to reach the nearest window. Flinging it open, she saw with relief that the rain and the wind had almost stopped, the clouds already dispersing.

Quickly she unscrewed the heavy helmet and pushed it back over Melvin's head, revealing his deathly pale face, drenched with perspiration. His eyes were closed; he was still breathing, but shallowly, like one in a coma. A sudden fear clutched at her heart. Leaving him, she hurried back to his office and called the Medical Department, where there was always someone on duty. In a few minutes a doctor came, followed by two attendants with a stretcher.

The doctor made a brief examination, then Melvin was lifted on to the stretcher and carried away down the corridor.

"Is—is it serious?" Lalia asked anxiously.

"No—but it might have been. Exposure to some kind of radiation, I fancy. At the same time, something went wrong with the air supply in his suit. What was it—some sort of experiment?"

She nodded. "I was watching outside—he said it might be dangerous. I saw him fall, so I went in and dragged him out into the corridor. I had to smash the door panel to do it."

The doctor glanced towards the open door of the laboratory. "I see. You scientists take too many risks. Better come along yourself—you've had a nasty shock. Lucky you didn't get burned...."

Too weak to argue, she went with him to the hospital bay where a nurse ministered to her. She had just drained a glass of sparkling restorative when the doctor returned from examining Melvin.

"He had better stay with us for a day or two," he told her. "He has recovered consciousness—"

"Can I see him?"

"Not for the moment, Miss Melbridge. He needs perfect quiet for the next few hours. He tells me you are his assistant in his research work. You'd better take these things of his—keys, identitygraph, and so on. You may need the keys, since he will be absent for a while."

Lalia nodded, signed for the belongings and put them in the pocket of her smock.

Slowly she made her way back towards the laboratory, her thoughts curiously muddled. Things had not gone at all as she had expected. There was something about Melvin's machine that mystified her more than ever—and about its creator. Did he intend that it should produce the effects it seemed to have done? Was he even more aware than he pretended of the devastating forces he sought to control, and which had only recoiled upon him in spite of his precautions? Why had he concealed so much from her? Was it to allay her fears for his safety, or—?

Suddenly she remembered that the laboratory door had been left unlocked.

Whatever his motives, she had vowed to keep his secret. It was unlikely that anybody remained in that part of the building at this hour, but if some unsuspected prowler had been waiting the opportunity— She quickened her pace until she reached the corridor where the door stood open, to find that her fears were groundless. All was deserted as before.

She stood for a time in the doorway, gazing meditatively at the great machine. But at last, thrusting her doubts aside, she turned to lower the steel shutter over the broken glass panel of the door, which Melvin had always kept in position to prevent even a glimpse of the machine from outside. She was just about to leave when she caught sight of a switch and wiring diagram, which Melvin had brought with him from his office, lying on a bench near the control board. She folded it and took it with her, locking the door as she left.

Returning to the office, she went to the safe and, after trying several keys, opened it and put the diagram inside. She had almost closed the heavy door when an inscription on the back of a rolled sheet of cartridge paper caught her eye. It was in Melvin's bold handwriting:

Thought Amplifier.

She stared, unbelieving. Surely Levison had not given him any of his designs? Then how had Melvin come by this one, if such it was? Unable to resist the temptation, she took out the roll of paper, slipped off the rubber band. The merest glance at the sheet, as she opened it out, was enough to assure her. It was undoubtedly a photostatic copy of the diagrams Levison had spread out on the bench in his workshop for his brother to inspect. They were all there. One or two of them were not very clear towards the bottom of the sheet, but on the whole the details were perfect, though the photographs seemed to have been taken at an angle that prevented a proper focus.

The conclusion was obvious—and unpleasant. As she rolled up the paper and replaced it in the safe, Lalia's face reflected the uneasy thoughts, which, this time, she could not banish. She stood there staring with unseeing eyes in which were only regret and misgiving. Then, with a sudden effort, she turned and ran from the office.

* * * * * * *

Two days later, Melvin was back at his desk. His curt summons for her to come to his office was the first intimation Lalia had of the fact. He looked up as she entered, his face expressionless.

"I believe Dr. Martin handed over to you several of my belongings, including my keys," he said shortly. "I would like them. It is a little—er—embarrassing having to rely on the commissionaire to let me into my own office."

She put the things on the desk. "I would have given them to you if I had known you were back," she remarked. "I called to see you, but they said—"

"I told them to tell you I was all right. I thought it better that we should not appear on too intimate terms. After all, you are one of my staff. Still, I'm nonetheless grateful for the way you rescued me. Undoubtedly, you saved my life."

She smiled faintly. "Something went wrong—"

"It was only my suit. You saw yourself how successful the test was. That's why I wanted you outside. I heard about it later, of course."

"You mean—the storm?"

"Precisely. I set out to produce those conditions through the machine. I succeeded—perhaps almost too well, after the suit went wrong and I lost control. A good job you had the sense to stop the machine— and to make things secure afterwards. However, we can take no more risks. I have decided to dismantle the machine and move it to my private laboratory, away from the Institute. We shall then be sure of perfect secrecy until we are ready to come out openly with a demonstration for the Master's benefit."

He paused as though waiting for her to say something, but she remained silent. He flashed a quick glance at her.

"You're sure that nobody saw into that laboratory? Dr. Martin, for instance?"

"Nobody. I locked up myself, and put the diagram you had out back in your safe."

She thought she saw a startled look pass swiftly across his features before he glared at her in sudden annoyance.

"You had no right to go to my safe, Lalia, even if Dr. Martin thought you were entitled to hold my keys! The diagram would have been quite secure where it was. Must I have you prying into all my secrets when my back is turned?"

She regarded him intently, ignoring the insult. He seemed uncomfortable beneath her cool, searching gaze. His indignation passed as quickly as it had come.

"I'm sorry, I shouldn't have said that. I have too much to thank you for. But, really, I don't like you taking such liberties, even if you are in my confidence."

She smiled, though her blue eyes were sad. "I understand," she murmured softly. "Now may I go back to my work?"

Long after she had gone, he sat staring after her, drumming nervous fingers on the desktop. Finally he got up and went to the safe.

* * * * * *

Within a fortnight the Elements Controller had been installed in Melvin's own laboratory, having been removed in sections and reassembled with Lalia's assistance. The underground compartment had been slightly enlarged to receive it, and the walls and ceiling so thickly reinforced by the workmen Melvin had engaged that Lalia was prompted to question the necessity for this added construction.

"Just to protect the machine, that's all," he told her in that casual manner with which he dismissed all her questions. "By the way," he went on, "I've seen the Master about a demonstration. He wants to see what we can do—tonight. I've promised to produce rain, hail, thunder, snow, and then a fine sunny evening, in that order."

"Indeed?" She tried to conceal her surprise. He had obviously left it to the last minute before he took her into his confidence. They were just completing the final stage of the machine's assembly.

He strolled to a corner cabinet, opened it to disclose two protective suits like the one he had worn the first time he tested the machine.

"You will be able to watch from inside this time. There will be no danger. I have seen to that."

He moved to the opposite wall, switched on the television periscope, which gave them visual contact with the surface. As he swept the light-photon magnetiser around at the turn of a dial, the whole landscape became visible in a panorama of distant green fields dotted with little dwellings, with part of the more densely packed outer ring of London looming in the foreground. At length they saw the great towered bulk of the city's centre rearing solid against the evening sky. The scanner turned full circle, and once more the screen showed a vista of peaceful fields and hollows huddling into the distance beyond the fringe of the city.

"We'll see if we can change all that," Melvin said, with one of his rare smiles.

Yet to Lalia, as she gazed in fascination at the screen, there was a lurking menace in his voice. She felt a little thrill of apprehension, if not actual fear, and glanced nervously about the laboratory, almost certain now that all was not as it should be. That great, shining machine which held the key to the mastery of the elements, and to much more than that for the cold, ruthless genius who had conceived its deadly power—it seemed to her a thing of latent evil, a grinning monster which had ensnared them both in its lair. And Melvin, the boy grown from ragged obscurity to the man she loved for his dogged perseverance and masterful nature, even if at times she doubted his motives; the man she had helped in his struggle, yet who regarded her as he might regard a piece of machinery— Here, deep beneath the surface, alone with him and his deadly powers, she was afraid—not of him, but of those powers he strove to control. She was afraid as much for him as for herself; perhaps a great deal more....

He seemed almost to sense her mood and tried to console her, not with comforting words or caresses, which were of no concern to hum, but with the promise of rewards which were his only criterion of value.

"You remember, Lalia, that when a little while ago we discussed the question of marriage I told you it would be better for us to wait until we had built this machine? But I said I would make you Mistress of Britain beside me once I had the power I had set out to get—to share that power with you in return for your help. If I succeed tonight in demonstrating that power—and I shall —you can hold me to that promise just as soon as you wish."

She forced herself to smile, to murmur her thanks, though she felt no enthusiasm at the prospect that had attracted her a year ago. She remained silent, staring into the screen and trying to stifle the qualms that tormented her, those fears that she had to convince herself were pure imagination. Until at length Melvin went to the cabinet and lugged out the two suits, began to clamber into one of them.

"It's nearly time," he told her. "Come on, get into this. These suits are equipped with audiophones, so we can talk to each other."

Mastering her uneasiness, Lalia obeyed. They checked their air supply carefully, then dropped the helmets in position. Melvin lumbered to the control board, threw in the main switch. The dynamos began to hum, meter needles jumped, and as he pulled another switch there was a sudden violent crackle of released energy and brilliant electric membranes leapt the gap between the globes.

From behind her tinted goggles, Lalia watched the mounting violence of that interchange of titanic energies. Even through her thick suit she felt the wafts of disturbed, heated air that eddied about her. But her timid fears were gone now. The deliberate efficiency with which Melvin operated the switchboard, as though to demonstrate to her his absolute mastery over the machine, reassured her completely, leaving her in rapt admiration of his superb confidence.

"Now!" he cried, and closed the big plunger switch connected with the distributor plant, into which the sizzling bolts of electric power had been hurling their terrific voltages. In a few seconds more the lavender beam came dimly into view, ascending to the concrete roof, and gradually deepening in colour and solidity. Enthralled, Lalia stood staring at it while Melvin waited, keeping careful watch on his meters. Eventually he looked up, and brought her out of her trance with a gesture towards the televisor behind her.

Lifting her goggles, she turned to look at the screen, to find the view strangely dimmed. Fifteen minutes before, it had been bright and sunny outside. Now it was dull and gloomy, the landscape barely discernible, overhung by thick black clouds. She turned the view control slowly, and the all-seeing eye traversed the surrounding vistas. Everywhere, in and outside the city, it was the same. Not a single ray of evening sun penetrated those darkly ominous masses of thundercloud floating above.

Again she felt that brooding fear, and turned to find Melvin gazing over her shoulder at the screen, his helmet pushed back over his head, eyes half-closed in a leer of smug satisfaction. Behind him that stabbing beam of lavender light was steady, unwavering.

"The—the storm!" she said uncertainly.

He nodded slowly, confidently. "It won't break yet," he assured her. "Meanwhile, perhaps I can satisfy your curiosity as to how this machine works. You know that the Sun is constantly throwing off streams of electrons, which enter the Earth's atmosphere and, under certain conditions, bring about electric storms. When an area of the atmosphere becomes impregnated with them, a positive electric field is built up, which finally discharges to earth.

"In just the same way, I can produce such storms with this machine by capturing and storing up those streams of electrons from the Sun and releasing them at will. This store of potential energy is the source of the vast power I use, of which I told you. When I have a potential of twenty billion solar volts, the energy is released from the storage globes and passed into the converters, thence to the distributor plant. It manifests itself in that violet beam and passes through to the outside just as easily as radio waves pass through solid substance. It reaches into the atmosphere, and there forms an intense positive field extending over a large area. Hence the dense thunderclouds produced by the change in atmospheric conditions. Eventually the charge breaks down, and we get our storm."

Lalia's doubts were not relieved by the knowledge of the machine's functioning. In fact, she was all the more certain that its purpose was merely to destroy.

"And what about the other conditions?" she ventured. "Or are you only interested in storms?"

He permitted himself a smile that was almost genuine. "At the moment, yes." Then his face hardened, his grey eyes grew cold, and his gloved hands clenched in grim determination. "I am going to produce a storm of such violence as has never been known in all history—a storm that will lay London, and all around it for a hundred miles, in the dust!"

Lalia's gnawing anxieties crystallised at last into a chilling panic which stopped her breath and clutched agonisingly at her heart. For an eternity she could only stand there staring, sick with horror, while she strove to find words with which to reply once she had recovered her power of speech.

"You—you don't mean—" Her tongue was still incapable of conveying her chaotic thoughts. Her lips trembled in sympathy with her shaking fingers. Melvin watched her stonily. There was deadly venom in his voice as he went on relentlessly.

"I mean that I am going to take my revenge on this proud city before I take its destinies into my hands. It needs a lesson—badly. When first I tried to gain a foothold in it, it despised me because of my lowly origin. I knew the ultimate power I sought, the Mastership of the city, would never be mine through ability alone. All through the years I have been constantly reminded that I was not born into the Intellectual Circle. So, to overcome that handicap, I produced this."

He waved a gloved hand towards the machine. There was a wild exultancy in his manner now, and his voice rose to a higher pitch. To Lalia, as she stood there transfixed, it sounded almost a shriek

"A destroyer—that's what it is, a destroyer of prejudices. And yet a creator—the builder of a new order of things. When I am Master, the city will see many changes. There will be plenty for us to do, Lalia!"

"You—you seem very sure—that you will be Master." The girl found the words a terrible effort. "If you're—found out—"

He laughed, hideously. "Oh, I've taken care of that! Rufus Latimer is in his office tonight—on the top floor of the highest building in the city. This storm will have no respect for tall buildings or for men of high office. It will be ruthless, devastating! In another ten minutes—"

Suddenly, to Lalia, this man she had cared for and encouraged stood revealed as a dangerous fiend armed with a dreadful weapon; a warped genius, drunk with ambition, who would stop at nothing to achieve his selfish ends. The realization brought her back to her senses, filled her with bitter anger that flowed through her veins in a flood of furious energy. Seized by a desperate impulse, she wheeled, snatched up a light steel chair, and flung it with all her strength at the posturing figure of Melvin.

He sensed her intention, but too late to do more than jerk his head aside. One of the tubular legs of the chair caught him full in the face, striking his forehead before it crashed to the floor. He raised a hand to his eyes, gave a little moan, swayed and crumpled up over the switchboard.

Lalia did not wait to see the result of her sudden burst of violence.

She was obsessed by one thought—to escape from

this crackling, stinking, blinding machine and the madman who had created it. As soon as she had flung the chair she turned to the door, pulled back the heavy bolts, swung it open and fled down the passage towards the steps which led up into the rear of the house. There she stopped only long enough to throw off her protective suit and snatch up her hat and coat. Then she ran to the front door and out into the roadway to her car parked on the side.

Gasping for breath, heart thumping wildly, she scrambled into it and drove off, snapping on the headlights as she pressed her foot hard on the accelerator. Though it was still early evening, the darkness was now almost as black as night itself; the rows of houses on either side were dotted lines of light, the road a shining ribbon of floodlit plastic stretching out ahead of her. The still air was warm and clammy; she was grateful for the gentle draught, which came through the lowered windows as the car gathered speed. A deathly silence, broken only by the soft purr of the wheels on the roadway, seemed to overhang the darkened world as though with a threat.

Now that she had escaped, she scarcely knew what to do or even where to go. She began to wonder if she should not go back to turn off the machine before it could do the damage Melvin intended. But she had not injured him seriously; he had probably recovered by now and would certainly prevent her interfering with his plans. In any case, the storm would break in a few minutes if what he had said was true. There was nothing she could do except try to save herself in the short time that remained.

If she tried to warn the people, who would heed her? And what could they do but await the storm they were already anticipating, without any suspicion of its unnatural origin, its catastrophic menace? Except, perhaps, Rufus Latimer. But by the time she reached the heart of London— She could only clutch at the hope that Melvin was exaggerating the potential violence of the storm. And yet....

Levison Read! The thought came to her as she realised that she was approaching a junction where the road to Paradise Acres led off on her left. She would go to him—he would understand. She would tell him the whole story of his brother's treachery, of her own foolish encouragement of his crazy lust for power. And if she could only get there in time, she might be able to warn him, to save him from the storm.

She drove madly until she reached the crossroads, turned and urged the car on at full speed. The road was clear, stretching out in a straight line of light towards the open country beyond the city's limits. The miles vanished beneath her racing wheels, until at last she topped the rise overlooking the little collection of bungalows lying in a green hollow. Then, abruptly, the storm broke.

A brilliant flash of lightning snaked across the black sky, piercing the gloom with a blinding intensity. Almost immediately a shattering crash of thunder shook the earth beneath with its terrific concussion.

Dazzled, Lalia clung to the steering wheel as the car dropped swiftly down the slope. The lightning came again, stabbing down from two directions in a shower of purple strands upon the road ahead. Even as she recoiled from the impact of the flash, the thunder beat at her eardrums, making her wince with pain; nor had she recovered from the shock of it before the road directly in front of her was again drenched with violet flame and the thunder rolled over her with mounting fury.

Another vivid flash forced her to lower her eyes from the windscreen for a fleeting instant. She raised them just in time to see a giant elm tree at one side of the road, fifty yards ahead, split itself in half and come toppling down across her path. She jammed on the brakes, came to a stop within two yards of its spreading branches which completely blocked the roadway. She clambered out of the car and stumbled forward through a lilac-tinted haze, reached the fallen tree as another blinding flash high above her was followed by a swishing roar as of a deadly projectile descending from the tortured skies. Startled, she looked up to see a ball of blazing brilliance fall into a distant meadow.

In the steady glare of the headlights and the cease-less lightning that dimmed them to pallid beams of yellow, she clawed her way between the branches of the fallen tree. While the thunder crashed on either side in a constant cannonade, she paused uncertain on the road beyond, peering into the intermittent gloom. Down there in the valley, dimly visible between the purple flashes, she could pick out the lights of houses in Paradise Acres. She still had the best part of a mile to go before she reached Levison Read's bungalow. A mile of terror, with lightning-swift death striking down at her every second.

She hesitated only a moment before she made up her mind. With sudden resolve, she made for the grass bank at the roadside, crawled between the wires of the fence, and started to walk across the field in the direction of the huddling houses. She had hardly taken half a dozen paces when the rain came, falling in huge drops which soon became a solid downpour, drenching her until her light overcoat was soaked, striking at her face and leaving her gasping, battling against its violence.

Then came the wind, sweeping across the field like a tornado, blowing her first to one side, then the other, and at times urging her forward as though in sympathy with her desperate desire for shelter. As she struggled on purposefully, the storm seemed only to increase its fury, the lightning descending in a brilliant cascade of violet that enveloped her in a flood of dazzling light that was at one with the torrential rain.

Then, through the flaming curtain that hemmed her in, a sudden, streaking flash struck at her like a sword. She staggered, screamed at the shock of the concussion, and fell headlong in the sodden grass.

For several minutes she lay there, paralysed, her whole body tingling, eyes staring helplessly at the sky, which presented a picture of awe-inspiring grandeur. Chain lightning rippled in an unholy filigree against a purple background, while here and there great, humped masses of jet-black cloud seemed to dilate and quiver as pent-up energies strained for outlet. When at length the numbness had gone out of her limbs, she got to her feet, stood for a moment gazing towards London.

A red glow hung over the city, visible even through the watery haze, while forks of savage brightness stabbed down into it ever and again with merciless insistence.

Set-faced, her heart pounding, she turned and went forward again. How she covered the remaining distance she hardly knew, but when at last the yellow oblongs of light loomed large before her she was filled with a deadly weariness, her head swimming from the incessant tumult of the storm, her eyes smarting from the wind and rain. She halted, breathless, a terrible ache in her side.

Then on again, until she half slid, half fell down a muddy, slippery bank to the flooded main road that ran through Paradise Acres.

Up to her knees in surging water, she struggled across towards the road that led to her destination, less than a quarter of a mile away. Again she was forced to stop while she regained sufficient energy to continue, clinging to the railings of a tiny house whose shattered roof testified to the damaging power of the storm. More than once, as she hurried on, she passed a house that had been reduced by a stroke of that incredibly vicious lightning to a heap of smouldering rubble. She breathed a prayer of infinite relief when at last she came to the little bungalow that was her final objective, to find it stood unharmed, its unshaded windows shining like welcoming beacons.

Thankfully she leaned for a second against the gate, then flung it open and ran up the path to the front door as another of those terrible lightning forks cleaved the sky above her. The ear-splitting burst of thunder was an overwhelming accompaniment to her frantic pounding on the door, which she continued as long as she had the strength. Then suddenly an awful weakness overcame her, she sagged helplessly against the door and collapsed in a heap on the step.

* * * * * * *

When she came to her senses, there was the sharp flavour of restorative in her mouth. The dinning chorus of thunder, howling wind, and swishing rain still assailed her ears, but seemed a little more remote, and the bright light around her shone steady and clear instead of in blinding bursts of violet. Gradually she became aware that she was lying comfortably on a low couch, at the foot of which a man stood smiling down at her.

"Levison!" She struggled up. "I thought I'd never get here—"

He pushed her gently back on her pillow, leaned over to make himself heard above the tumult outside.

"Take it easy for now. You've had a pretty rough journey. My housekeeper, Mrs. Dawson, fixed you up and took off your wet things. Just now she's in the kitchen getting some tea."

Lalia glanced down at the warm blankets that covered her. "I'm very grateful. I was about all in. I think I fainted."

She buried her head in the pillow as a tremendous crack of thunder shook the house to its foundations, and opened her eyes to find Levison regarding her coolly. She almost screamed at him:

"Don't you realize this place may be struck at any moment? I've passed several smashed houses—and London is in flames. If this terrible storm goes on through the night—"

She paused as the elderly Mrs. Dawson came in with tea on a tray. She smiled at Lalia, set down the tray, and went out again with apparent unconcern. Levison passed the cup to her.

"Now, just drink this and go to sleep —if you can. We can talk later."

She was too exhausted to protest. Though the storm still raged, there was something about the calm assurance of Levison Read that gave her a sense of security, dissolving her useless fears. She returned the cup, sank back again on her pillow, closed her tired eyes.

When she awoke, Levison was standing by the window, through which the first faint rays of the morning sun were shining into the room. The only sounds were the steady drip of water from the choked gutters of the eaves and the tinkle of china in the kitchen.

"The storm—when did it pass?" she asked anxiously.

Levison turned. Despite his smile, there was a look almost of horror in his eyes.

"It lasted nearly six hours. Then it ceased as suddenly as it began. Such fury! It must be unprecedented. I can't make it out. Unless—"

She sat up. "I came to tell you. It was Melvin's work—and mine. I feel I'm as much to blame for the havoc it must have caused. I helped him to build the machine...."

He listened patiently while she told him, right from the beginning. If he felt any surprise, he did not reveal it. He did not even flinch when she told him how she had found the plans of his Thought Amplifier in Melvin's safe. She told him of her own constant suspicions and how she had repeatedly dismissed them from her mind; how her admiration for Melvin had proved stronger than her mistrust. Until, now that he had revealed himself as a vindictive ingrate whose sole object was to satisfy his mad lust for power, her affection for him had turned to bitter hatred and disillusionment.

"He's a dangerous man, Levison," she insisted, finally. "A genius, yes, but an utterly unscrupulous one. If he becomes Master of London, it can only end in slavery and misery for the people. He would be a ruthless tyrant, and he won't rest until he has the whole world in his grip. Unless he can be stopped—"

Levison Read only smiled, though there was still that look of deep concern in his eyes.

"He's more of a fool than anything," he said quietly.

"I might have known he was responsible for this. But he won't get very far with his terror and destruction. There have been other fools...."

* * * * * * *

Slowly Melvin Read turned away from the visi-screen, unfastened the clips of his heavy insulated suit, and stepped out of its protecting folds. For a moment he stood regarding the massive machine, now silent and inactive, its deadly work complete. He grimaced as he sniffed the heavy, stale air in the laboratory; then he turned to the door, opened it, and went swiftly along the passage. He climbed the steps, passed through the house into the cool atmosphere outside. He noticed that his own dwelling had not escaped the damaging effects of the storm, but it had not fared too badly.

A fresh wind was blowing from the east. The last clouds of the great storm were drifting westwards like a retreating armada, dead black against the grey dawn sky. Keenly he surveyed the landscape, and as his gaze settled on the soft, red glow reflected above the centre of the city, a smile came slowly to his lips.

He'd done it. In spite of Lalia's crazy attack on him, her foolish treachery, he had done what he had set out to do. He had lain there dazed for some time after she had fled, and had come to his senses to find the machine still running, the storm almost at its height. For hours he had watched it through the television periscope, exulting in its terrible abandon, its wild, flashing fury. Until at last, content, he had stopped the machine and the tempest had gradually subsided, leaving him to contemplate the havoc it had caused over the whole area of the city and beyond.

But it was not enough to remain there, concealed, viewing his handiwork from a distance. He could not resist the temptation to go out into the streets to see the devastation he had wrought at close quarters, to see the effect on the city's inhabitants of this catastrophe whose true nature they had yet to learn. He had given them an abundant demonstration of his power. When he was their Master they would respect him all the more for that. But first he must seize the Mastership; they would not know until later that the storm was not a natural phenomenon, if an unprecedented one.

Lalia, of course, would talk—if she still survived. If she was dead, so much the better. He had been a fool to trust her as far as he did. But she had been useful. Now he could forget her.

He drove the car out of the underground garage and along the road, still flooded from the deluge. Making towards the city's centre, he soon gained a closer, grimmer perspective of the disaster he had created. Crumpled villas, fallen trees, swirling waters covered with driftwood, presented a picture of widespread destruction in the outer circle of the city.

It grew lighter as he came nearer to the inner section, where he was forced to abandon the car and proceed on foot to observe the utter chaos that revealed itself in the battered streets. Everywhere he looked he saw tangled girders and shattered masonry where tall, stately buildings had stood. Commercial Tower had gone, felled by the merciless lightning. The Science Institute had suffered, one wing a great pile of broken concrete and twisted steel. The Weather Bureau and the Ambassadors' Building were only two of the blackened, smoking shells left by devouring flames, which even the rain had failed to quench. Elsewhere, in many parts of the city, fires were still raging, defying the weary, grimy men who still strove to defeat them.

Through the streets, too, wandered little aimless groups of men, women, and children who had been driven from the wreckage of their homes; while others were curious sightseers, gazing stupefied at scenes of devastation and horror. Rescue squads worked ceaselessly amid tumbling ruins. Ambulances raced, bells ringing wildly, or stood vigilantly by while sullen bulldozers shoved aside debris. As Melvin neared the city's shattered heart, the activity increased.

"Terrible, isn't it?"

He turned sharply. A stocky, well-built man with tousled hair and dirty, perspiring face stood at his elbow. There was bitter sorrow in his eyes; his mouth was shut tight as though in an effort to master his emotion. His clothes were torn, and he held his left arm in a rude sling beneath his empty sleeve.

"Pretty bad," Melvin admitted almost grudgingly. Somewhere within him was a strange feeling of discomfort, which he had been trying to analyse even as he strove to conquer it. It was not remorse—it could only be nausea. He had no regrets. He had set out to accomplish this, and he had succeeded. For him it was triumph, not tragedy. Yet now he could feel none of that splendid satisfaction he had tasted when he first surveyed the landscape from the laboratory. The finer details were a little—distasteful.

"I was in a holo-cinema with my wife and two kiddies," the man said absently. "We heard thunder, but thought nothing of it. Then the whole place caved in. My wife and kids were crushed under a steel girder. They got me out. I wish they hadn't...."

"I'm sorry." Melvin wanted to get away from him, but the man suddenly grasped his arm with his free hand as though anxious to unleash his feelings now that he had found someone who would listen.

"I can't understand it, can you?" he went on. "That storm—it was no ordinary storm, was it? It couldn't have been. There's never been another like it. I wonder—"

He broke off, peering into Melvin's face. "I'm sure I've seen you somewhere before, haven't I? At the Science Institute, perhaps—"

Melvin smiled faintly, threw off his morbid feelings. There was no reason why he should conceal his identity. The whole of London would know him soon enough. His name would be on every lip.

"I'm Melvin Read," he said. "Vice-Chief of the Electronic Department."

"Why, of course!" The man brightened, held out his hand. "I'm Curtis Townsend, engineer. We must have met. I often have business at the Institute. I knew

Mernas Steele very well. Latimer, too."

Melvin frowned, feigning surprise. "You *knew* them? You mean—"

"You haven't heard? It was on the radio and TV. All stations broke down when the storm was on, but they've got going again. They're putting out bulletins, they tell me. The death roll's estimated at ten thousand, maybe more. Several big names among the missing, the Master and Chief Scientist included. They're dead for certain—no trace."

Melvin's pulses raced. It was just what he had hoped for. Now was his opportunity.

"Then the city's without a leader, a central authority. There will have to be an election," he urged.

Townsend's face was blank. "In time, I suppose. The administration's still functioning as best it can, but it will take weeks to clear up this mess. Someone will have to shoulder the responsibility in the meantime. It's no light task—"

"I'll take it on." Melvin's voice was challenging, though he tried to conceal his eagerness. "I was next to Mernas Steele, have all the qualifications. If things are left to the petty officials, they will all be quarrelling among themselves and nothing will be done. The people must have a leader, someone whose word is law and whom they can trust, or they will get out of hand. If I speak to them, I'm sure they will put me in that position until we can have a proper election. If you and your friends will give me your support and nominate me, I shall not easily forget it."

Townsend ruminated, his personal grief forgotten in his concern for the city's welfare. He had heard of this Melvin Read in the influential circles in which he was privileged to move, even if he did not strictly belong to them. Men spoke his name, he remembered, with something of envy and respect, while treating him as an inferior. Perhaps if he threw in his lot with him....

"There's something in what you say, and I admire your public spirit," he confessed. "Of course, I'm only an engineer—"

"And the very man I want to have charge of the rebuilding of the city," Melvin encouraged.

"Then you can count on my full support. Come along to my office, and we'll see if we can get you on the TV and radio once we've got your nomination through. The people will acclaim you—I've no doubt of that. Yes, Melvin Read for Master it shall be!"

* * * * * * *

The reaction of the people to Melvin's appointment as temporary Master was enough to show their willingness to accept any leader who could inspire them with the courage and determination that were most needed in the present emergency. The harassed administration welcomed him as one who was prepared to relieve them of the burden of responsibility in a crisis they could not cope with; and those of the Intellectual Circle who were loath to accept him were at least prepared to grant him the extra burdens of his office while they lasted. Later, when he had reorganised affairs sufficiently for an election to be held, he could be easily deposed by a candidate more to their liking.

But Melvin Read, having grasped his opportunity, was quick to exert his new power in a way that would ensure his retention of it. He spared no pains to persuade the people that he alone could give them the betterments they craved by his ruthless domination of the whole community and its resources of capital and labour. Within a few days, the city's three hundred thousand homeless had been given fresh shelter, and the work of repairing the tens of thousands of damaged homes and buildings had begun, under the direction of Townsend. With prospects of such a swift rehabilitation, the people's hopes rose as they demonstrated their confidence in the new leader.

But he, conscious of the precariousness of his position, knew he could not rely on fickle popularity to defeat the more subtle forces arrayed against him. If his bid for power failed, he must resort once more to the Elements Controller, that master bargaining weapon, which would always be more valuable than votes. At the same time, it was imperative that the secret of the machine be kept. Beneath the ruins of his home it was safe enough, but he had to have access to its violent strength at all times, against any emergency.

Only he knew the purpose of the complicated switchboard that was promptly installed in his office in the Science Institute, where he made his temporary headquarters until the rebuilding of Commercial Tower. Much less did those few who were aware of its existence realize that behind it was an ingenious remote control apparatus which enabled him to operate the Elements Controller with the same facility as if he were in the underground laboratory where it was concealed.

But the precaution proved unnecessary. When, within two months, he was forced to accede to the demands of those who opposed him and submit himself for election, the people clamoured for him to remain in office rather than accept any of his rival nominees. His forthright methods, coupled with his assurances of continued progress to benefit Intellectuals and Workers alike, had brought him general approval, and he found himself with the Mastership for a further period of two years.

Engineer Townsend was the first to call at his office on the morning after the election.

"You deserve it, Read," he said warmly. "You've done wonders. The people want a man of action."

"You've done well, too," Melvin acknowledged. "But we still have to move faster. We need more labour. The other cities can't or won't co-operate, so what we can't get from outside we must get from within. We shall have to be ruthless. My first act will be to conscript everybody within a hundred miles radius into the Workers' Circle, to help with the rebuilding."

Townsend raised his black brows. "That's not going to be very popular, is it?"

"Perhaps not. But I want to see this city rebuilt— and quickly. We need more houses for the workers, and until they have them we shall never make progress on the bigger schemes for which we are all impatient. The whole of the city is too crowded. I want to see it expand still further into the countryside. The inner circle will be enlarged to the present limits of the outer circle, which will spread out beyond that. We shall absorb the small towns and the few villages that are left, cover the fields with houses, keep such open spaces as are necessary. London needs more territory—and more Workers. There are too many Intellectuals. You understand?"

The engineer looked doubtful, but he nodded. "You want me to get started on this expansion scheme?" he asked.

"Very soon. Of course, it will take time. But we shall work as fast as we can—keep the people occupied. Meanwhile, I have other plans which do not concern you."

"I see." Townsend lowered his gaze. "Well, you can rely on me."

As the door closed behind the engineer Melvin Read sat back in his chair, musing. His pensive eye lighted on the wall-safe where the plans of Levison's Thought Amplifier still reposed, neglected but not forgotten. In the two months that had passed he had heard nothing of his brother, nor of Lalia. Perhaps they had both died. She, at least, would surely have come to him in the hour of his triumph, asking his forgiveness, wanting to share his success. He had to make certain, now, that he was rid of her. And of Levison....

* * * * * *

The man in the dark grey uniform, standing at the door of the bungalow, announced his business in a tone that brooked no argument.

"You are instructed to come with me to London immediately for essential employment in the Workers' Circle. Here is my authority."

Levison Read took the paper the officer held out to him.

"You understand," he emphasised, "you are to come immediately. Accommodation will be provided for you. This house and your belongings will be taken care of by the authorities until your services are dispensed with, but it will be necessary for you to live with the Workers for the time being. Bring with you only the things you need—"

"But what is this?" Levison found his voice. "Emergency Order? Recruitment of labour?"

"If you don't come willingly I shall have to arrest you," the officer threatened. "The vehicle is waiting just along the road. You won't be the only one. I'll expect you there in ten minutes."

He was about to turn on his heel when he caught sight of the girl coming into the passage. His eyes raked her.

"Your wife?" He leered.

Lalia answered before Levison could speak, giving her name and explaining that she was staying at the bungalow because her own apartments had been destroyed in the Great Storm.

"Lalia Melbridge, eh? Lucky for me. I've been

looking for you, Miss Melbridge. Two birds with one stone."

He searched through his papers, handed her a document similar to the one he had given Levison. "You'll have to come along too." He winked heavily at Levison. "If you're good, perhaps they'll fix you up together. Don't forget—ten minutes."

He was gone. Lalia looked up from the paper, her blue eyes puzzled.

"But this is absurd! If this is some of Melvin's work—"

"He doesn't waste any time, does he?" said Levison. "So the Intellectuals must become Workers, by order of the Master! He's running his head into trouble already. But we'd better get ready."

Lalia's frown turned to a look of complete bewilderment. "You—you mean you're going? Under threats? You're going to let him force you to give up your work on the Amplifier? That's just what he wants—"

"If we refuse we shall only be playing into his hands, giving him an excuse to put further pressure on us. It won't hurt us to live in the Workers' Circle for a while. It will give me a chance to protest against his high-handed actions—to meet him face to face if I can. Yes, I think we'd better go."

She was still inclined to doubt when they took their seats in the great three-decker motor-bus outside, into which many others like themselves were climbing, carrying suitcases and parcels of intimate belongings. But she knew it was useless to resist. For the moment,

Melvin had the whip hand. They would have to bide their time.

The bus stopped once to pick up a little group of people waiting at the roadside with two grey-uniformed men, then continued on its way towards London. The passengers were silent, uneasy; there were a few feeble protests, but no more. The officers were grimly uncommunicative. The prospect looked bleak.

The bus reached the outer city traffic levels, entered the drab regions of the Workers' Circle with its rows of little grey houses. They passed many ugly spaces littered with the debris of those that had been torn down, either by the storm itself or in consequence of its toll of damage. In every street gangs of workmen toiled at the task of reconstruction. Eventually the bus pulled up outside a public building. The officers herded them out, up the wide steps and into a queue which trailed through the great hall to a door labelled 'Registrations'.

When at length they reached the table where a flint-faced official sat ready to ply them with questions in their turn, Levison spoke up:

"I wish to appeal against this treatment. I am engaged on important work."

The official glared. "There is no work more important than the rebuilding of the city. The Master has ordered that you shall be engaged in such work, at least until you can be spared for less urgent matters. No appeals against that decision are permitted. Your name, please!"

"Levison Read. The Master is my brother—"

"That makes no difference. Kindly reply to the questions.... Occupation?"

Levison hesitated, seemed as though he would carry his protest further, then gave up the struggle with a shrug. He made his replies mechanically, moved aside to make way for Lalia. The officer ignored the defiance in her voice as she gave her particulars. At the end he looked up and announced to all and sundry:

"If there is anybody who feels inclined to question the Master's judgment in this matter, may I remind them that the Master has the right under the Act of Mastership to make whatever order he chooses in an emergency, without reference to any other authority. Next, please!"

* * * * * * *

It was only by degrees that Levison and Lalia came to realize how completely Melvin's edict had them in its grip. They were given billets fairly close to each other and put to work in the same underground factory; there were ample facilities for recreation, and as long as they were content to adapt themselves to their new mode of life they were not interfered with. But they were under constant surveillance by the grey-uniformed police who patrolled the Workers' Circle night and day, ensuring that they did not pass the jealously guarded barriers into the city's inner circle without a special permit. To impress upon them even further their loss af Intellectual status, they were obliged to wear the drab olive-green dress of the Workers at all times.

By patient application to the proper authority, Levison gained permission to retrieve the apparatus and equipment he needed to continue work on the Thought Amplifier in his periods off duty, and the little room which Lalia visited every evening soon had all the appearance of his Paradise Acres workshop, except for its cramped dimensions. Though greatly handicapped, he laboured more diligently than ever, while Lalia helped where she could. But as the days lengthened into weeks and their enforced duties in the factory grew more and more irksome, she grew impatient, resentful.

"We've got to do something, Levison," she told him yet again. "We're just letting Melvin have all his own way. While he has you chained down here, working only when you're free from your factory bench, you will never do the job before him. For all we know, he may have this thing practically finished. And when once he starts to use it—"

Levison looked up from the delicate piece of apparatus to which he was making adjustments.

"We're very lucky to be able to work on it all, Lalia," he reminded her patiently. "Don't forget we're not the only ones to have our work interrupted. At the bench next to me at the factory is a professor of physics—"

"I know!" Lalia had grown tired of his attempts to console her. "But Melvin may not even know we're alive. Some official must have put our names down on that list of Intellectuals who have been turned into menial Workers—slaves, in fact; for that's all we are, all we ever shall be. There are thousands of us, all doomed to this existence for the rest of our lives if Melvin gets his way. But if he knew we were here, he might have the decency to reinstate us."

"And let us work on the Amplifier, which he wants to use for his own ends? You know that's not reasonable, Lalia. We've been here two months. If he thought we were alive, he would have sought us out by now. At least, he'd have seen to it that I wasn't allowed to continue my work here. I'd have been refused permission. No, it's best to let things stay as they are."

Lalia's eyes flashed. "How do you know he isn't doing it deliberately—letting you get on with the job while all the time he's got you tied down? When you've finished the Amplifier, he'll step in and confiscate it. We're helpless either way. If only we could find out how much he knows, how far he's made progress!"

"I think we should wait, Lalia." he insisted gently.

But she could wait no longer. She could not bear to see Levison toiling night after night, getting no rest, when all his efforts might be in vain. She had to see Melvin, to find out the truth. He need never know that Levison lived, if he thought him dead, She could delude him; perhaps persuade him, in spite of what had happened, to reinstate her so that she could use her influence to get Levison released from his slavery without Melvin's knowledge.

Her mind made up, she did not hesitate. Leaving Levison to his labours as early as she could without exciting his suspicions, she made her way through the deserted, ill-lighted streets towards the narrow belt of grassland that separated the inner rim of the Workers' Circle from the centre of the city. Soon she came to one of the great portals through which all traffic entering the inner section filtered to the various levels, and where a pedestrian was such a rarity that only a single narrow subway on either side of the towering arch had been provided for foot passengers, as though as an afterthought. Beyond the portal, a flood of light from the great city buildings, resplendent with flashing sky-signs, reached into the heavens to put the stars to shame.

As she drew nearer the subway entrance, Lalia searched in vain for some suggestion of shadow in which she night escape the mechanical eyes of the. grey-uniformed police who made their vigil here, ever watchful lest some unauthorised Worker attempt to enter the forbidden precincts of the city. But it was impossible to gain the subway without passing their observation posts, smooth domes of shining plastic from whose summits revolving lights swept the footway with their merciless beams. Once she stepped into that light they would see the olive-green uniform that marked her as a Worker, and a Worker had to be questioned. It was unavoidable.

For a moment Lalia stopped, blinking at the whirling rays of light, and wondered if she should not wait until she could obtain a permit to enter the city on some legitimate errand. But the formality would take time; the document would require her Overseer's signature. It was all designed to discourage Workers from encroaching on the rightful preserves of the Intellectuals. She had to see Melvin now—that night; he would almost certainly be working in his office in the Science Institute. She would get there somehow.

She continued towards the subway, whose dim inner lights seemed poorer still against the bright glare outside. She almost ran, knowing that if the men in the observation post saw she was in a hurry they would keep her waiting longer at the turnstile before they started their interrogation. Just before she reached the viewplate, which would present her life-size image to them inside the post, a mechanical voice grated:

"Halt! Stand by for questioning."

But she did not halt. Instead she plunged forward into the ill-lit subway and, keeping as close to the wall as she could, ran faster than she had ever done in her life before. She had gone ten yards when the robot voice repeated: "Halt! Stand by—" Then a human voice commanded, "Stop, or I'll shoot!" as she heard the clatter of heavy boots behind her: someone inside the post must have moved as fast as she.

She was almost on the point of staying her headlong progress down the straight, narrow tunnel when something blazed behind her, a fierce burst of pain racked her spine, and she fell into a pit of absolute blackness.

* * * * * * *

Lalia had been gone less than an hour when Levison

Read was startled by a sudden peremptory knocking on the door of the billet. He was alone in the house; the others always spent their evenings at the Recreation Centre. Hurriedly he pushed aside the apparatus on which he was working, and went downstairs to the door. A man in Workers' Hospital uniform stood waiting. There was a car in the road outside.

"Levison Read?" he asked briefly, then went on at the other's nod. "A girl named Melbridge was shot by the police while trying to pass the barrier without permission. She's in hospital, in a pretty bad way—gave your name. You can come with me."

As the car sped through the narrow streets, Levison's mind was an agonizing muddle of hope, fear, and regret. The few minutes before he was standing at Lalia's bedside, looking down at her white face, seemed an interminable age.

"Only a moment," the nurse cautioned as she left them.

"Hello, Levison." The girl's whisper was almost inaudible. "I—I tried to see Melvin—but they stopped me—"

Bitter anguish showed in his eyes as he leaned over the bed. "Whatever made you do it, Lalia? I would have gone myself if I'd thought—" The words choked him. He could only gaze at her, tenderly.

"Never mind," she whispered. "You know best. If—if I don't get better. I want you to know that I'm still on your side."

He nodded dumbly. She lay staring up at him until

the nurse intervened.

A moment later, in the corridor outside, he realized dimly that a doctor was speaking to him.

"We operated the moment she was brought in. We saved her life, but there is a bad spinal injury. She will probably find it difficult to walk again...."

Levison wandered out into the street in a daze. Never to walk again—

Involuntarily, his fists clenched. This was another piece of Melvin's hateful work. Lalia was right—they had to throw off these shackles he had put upon them, to prevent him doing them further injury. He had to show him that with all his power he could not succeed in his crazy scheme of domination.

He had to match that power with his own—now.

The numbness passed from his shocked mind, gave place to a burning sense of injustice, which flared into a raging fury towards his brother. Spurred to sudden activity, he swung round, hurried back into the hospital forecourt where a small autogyro stood parked.

Keeping well in the shadow, his eye on the solitary figure in the light of the main entrance, he opened the door, slipped into the seat, set the vanes revolving as soon as he heard the first soft purr of the engine.

The man in the doorway turned, stared out into the gloom, waved a hand wildly and came running across the forecourt towards the plane. Levison waited until he was three yards away, then opened the throttle wide. With a lurch that turned his stomach, the plane leapt straight up into the air.

He turned on the jets, climbed swiftly up above the hospital roof, and stilled the whirring helicopter as he brought the machine round towards the blaze of light marking the city's centre. Within seconds he hung suspended over its twinkling abysses. He peered down, searching; it was a long time since he had piloted his own gyro over London, but at last he made out the expansive roof of the Science Institute. He nosed down towards it, hovered motionless above it for a moment, then let the plane down to a gentle landing on the rooftop where several other tiny machines were parked.

He went down in the lift without encountering a watchman. The corridors were silent, deserted, though lights still burned here and there. He found an indicator, located Melvin's office on the third floor. The glass panel of the door glowed with light. He pushed the door open, went through the outer office to where another door stood ajar. He flung it open.

Melvin looked up with a start from the desk where he was studying a sheet of diagrams. At his side lay several pieces of apparatus, which were not unfamiliar to Levison. The blood drained slowly from the Master's face as he sat there staring at the visitor in the olive-green uniform. At length he spoke.

"I—I thought you must be dead. I hadn't heard—"

"You could have found out easily enough, couldn't you?" Levison put the question calmly. His rage was gone now, leaving only grim determination. "The Master surely should be aware of all his citizens' welfare,

Intellectuals and Workers alike. It might interest you to know that Lalia Melbridge also survived the storm—and that she now lies in a Workers' Hospital, paralysed by the shock-ray of one of your henchmen. She was trying to get to you, to plead with you, even though she now realizes what a cold-blooded monster you are."

Uneasily Melvin rose from the desk, forced himself to meet the other's challenging gaze. With an obvious effort he made his excuses.

"She attacked me in my laboratory, left me unconscious. If she had only approached me in the proper way I might have overlooked that. If she chooses to defy law and order, I cannot be held responsible."

"Law and order!" Levison's tone was not so cool. "Who are you to speak of such things? You who seek to thrive on violence—yes, and on thievery!" He waved a hand towards the apparatus on the desk. In a renewed burst of uncontrollable anger, he dived forward, swept it to the floor and ground its shining complexities beneath his feet.

Melvin's eyes gleamed hateful enmity. He tensed his body, hurled himself at his brother, fingers crooked like talons. But Levison was quicker. Flinging out an arm, he sent him staggering back on to a low settee where he sat panting, glowering.

"You'll pay for this," he growled. "You can't attack the Master. I'll have you taught a lesson. I have the power—"

"Power!" The word came back like a boomerang. "Power! The power to destroy! Too much of that will bring you down before long, Melvin. You can't control it—"

"But I can!"

Melvin leapt to his feet as he shrieked his defiance. Levison backed away, then stood his ground, awaiting a second plunge. But instead of attacking him again, Melvin stepped aside, round the settee, and ran to the other side of the room where a shiny black panel stood out from the surface of the wall. He touched a button, slid the panel aside to disclose an array of switches and dials.

"You see! I have my power ready to hand—the power that put me here and will keep me here so long as I choose! Unlimited power! You've already seen what the release of that power can do, Levison. The Great Storm that almost destroyed London—it was I who caused it. And I can do it again!"

He was raving now, drunk with wild exultancy. Levison watched him, half contemptuous, half pitying.

"You shall see!" With a hoarse cry, Melvin slammed down a great switch on the panel, started to turn a dial while he kept a careful eye on Levison. "If you and Lalia try to get me removed, the whole of London will answer for it. Better think again, Levison. If you would only co-operate with me—"

He stopped and stared as he became aware that someone lurked just outside the office door, looking straight at him through the gap where it had been pushed partly open. Levison could see only a vague shadow behind the glass. Then slowly the door swung back, revealing a stocky, muscular figure standing on the threshold

"Townsend!" Melvin's face whitened visibly, stark against the blackness of the switchboard. For a moment he struggled in indecision, laid a hand on the panel as though to though to close it, then let it fall to his side. He stood silent, lips twitching nervously eyes shifting from Levison to Townsend and back again.

Townsend's tone was confident, commanding. "Release that switch!" he ordered.

Melvin hesitated again. He made a terrific effort to regain his composure hunching back his shoulders, head held high.

"Who are you to give orders to the Master?" he demanded. "You had no permission to enter my office."

The engineer moved forward purposefully. He had reached the switchboard before Levison caught sight of the vibragun in his hand. Brushing Melvin aside, he reached up with the other, opened the switch, and turned to face them both. He gestured with the gun towards Levison, then levelled it straight at Melvin's breast.

"This man—your brother—didn't wait for permission either. His errand was too important. So is mine—now. I was coming to see you on a matter that is too trifling to mention—it can wait. I hadn't long landed in my gyro and was digging out some papers when this man touched down on the roof. I saw his Worker's uniform, followed him down to your office. When I first saw his face I thought it was you, though I couldn't understand the dress. When I heard you talking, I learned differently. I learned a lot of things—things that have been troubling me for some time but which I couldn't fit together before."

His tone was quietly conversational now. Melvin stood glaring at him, his chest heaving rhythmically, while Levison watched impotently. The stocky man went on.

"I always knew there was something funny about that storm. There was that beam of violet light that some were supposed to have seen, which led to talk of invaders from space—absolute nonsense! Lots of people had theories—all sorts of fantastic ideas, which they put over the radio and TV. But I never could accept the scientists' verdict that it couldn't be anything but a natural phenomenon. It was too restricted, too concentrated. There never was a storm like that, and there never will be again."

He looked at Melvin with narrowed eyes as he spoke the last few words, slowly and deliberately. He glanced quickly at Levison, then resumed in a voice that trembled slightly.

"I lost my wife and youngsters, all I had, in that storm. Thousands died and suffered through it, and are still suffering—because of you, Melvin Read. I was a fool to let you use me in your climb to power, but I'm not the only one you've used for your own ends, it seems. This apparatus—" He nodded towards the broken pieces on the floor, turned to Levison again. "It's some invention he's filched from you. It must be important. What is it exactly?"

Levison told him, briefly. Melvin's face showed dull resentment. Twice he made an effort to speak, but each time Townsend silenced him abruptly.

"The power to influence men's minds...." The engineer considered, his gaze wandering aimlessly for a moment. Then he smiled grimly at the Master. "To think what you would have done with that! But your reign of terror's at an end, Melvin Read. You'll never be able to satisfy your conscience, perhaps, but I'm going to do what I can to still mine. We put one Master in power. Now we'll replace him with another—one with rather different motives, if I'm any judge. And without any formalities or elections, either. What do you say, Levison Read?"

Levison was startled by the sheer audacity of the notion. "You mean that I should take Melvin's place? I don't want power—"

"You *have* the power! You can work miracles with that invention. Your brother's crazy lust for it is enough indication of that. But he wants to destroy—you want to build, to cure. Well, now's your chance!"

He spoke rapidly, urgently. "When I entered this room, I tell you, I did so with the intention of shooting this blackguard down where he stood, not only for what he's done to me but to avenge the thousands he's sinned against. He deserves to die—and I'm still tempted to give him what he deserves, even if you try to stop me. But it will do me no good—I'd have to pay the penalty or blow my own brains out. There'd be a scandal; the people would lose what little faith they have left in the Master, and our enemies would make the most of it.

"You're his twin. He must go—you have all the qualifications that are needed. If you stepped into his shoes, we could go on as if nothing had happened, except that you'd take a different line. The people would accept you; our opponents would never know. You'd have me to stand by you—"

Levison's mind was a turmoil of confused thoughts. "But—but Melvin—"

Townsend waved his gun. Melvin nervously watched his every movement. He was thoroughly frightened now. He clutched at the chance desperately.

"Yes—yes, take my place, Levison! You deserve it. So does Lalia. I know when I'm beaten—I'll go away."

"Take off your clothes," Townsend told him. "Levison, give him your Workers' uniform."

Silently, while the engineer watched, the brothers exchanged clothes. Neither of them saw the peculiar smile that flickered briefly on Townsend's lips.

* * * * * * *

The Master of London raised his eyes from his desk, gazed through the huge window at the skeleton fingers of metal, which pointed upwards, here and there, between the network of girders and the mass of newly-finished buildings below. He nodded approvingly to himself, leaned back in his chair and sat reflecting. The city wasn't such a bad place, after all. And it would be better still....

A glow of light suffused the audio-screen on the desk, rousing him from his reverie. A voice announced: "Miss Melbridge." Levison responded briefly, eagerly. In a moment Lalia was in the room.

"I had to see you," she said, her blue eyes shining. "The visor is so— impersonal."

"I'm glad you came," he replied. "Did you see— him?"

Her eyes clouded. There was sadness in her voice. "It was all I could do to persuade him, but he finally agreed to place himself in Dr. Seldon's hands. I told him what the Thought Amplifier had done for me, how it had fulfilled all your expectations in curing hundreds of cases of disease by influencing the mind. He tried to convince me that his case was different, said the principle didn't apply where the tissues had been damaged by harmful radiations such as those from his machine. If he had thought at the time, he said, that his exposure to them might have such an effect after three months, he would have taken steps to ward it off. But it was only recently he began to suspect that his brain had been affected while he lay there in the laboratory unconscious, without his helmet, on the day of the Great Storm.

"I pleaded with him, told him I felt I was to blame for having left him there exposed to those deadly radiations. But he insisted it was his own fault for meddling with forces that he couldn't properly control. He was a little hysterical—he's very ill, Levison. He realises, now, in spite of his growing madness, that his craving for power and his misuse of it once he had it in his grasp could only bring about his downfall. He's completely penitent—and wretched."

Levison looked anxious. "But he did agree to submit himself to the Amplifier?"

"He said he would try it, if only for my sake, so that I would have nothing on my conscience. Though he insisted I shouldn't have, and that he didn't deserve to escape—his penalty, he called it. Since he first realized his illness soon after he went away, he's been resigned to his fate, waiting for it. He thought of killing himself, but he said he hadn't the courage—the courage that you had, Levison.

"He was full of admiration for you and what you have accomplished. The rebuilding, the replanning, the abolition of the Workers' Circle, their equal status—he praised them all. You had a sense of rightness he could never have, he said. And your scheme for the universal acceptance of the Amplifier, to rid men's minds of fear and mistrust and to promote the ideals of human progress—he was all in favour of that, too. He's a changed man, if a hopeless one."

She brightened. "But Melvin will live," she added confidently. "The Amplifier will heal his brain and restore his mind, just as it will improve the minds of millions, stop all the muddled thinking and prejudice that hold us back. It's a perfect instrument for good, Levison. With it, we can remake the world. Or you can—for as you've always said, the responsibility lies with you."

He got up from the desk, stopped to stare once more through the window at those gleaming fingers pointing towards the sky. He turned to her, smiling.

"Let's try together, shall we?" he said.

NEMESIS

The edifice of the World Council was packed to the doors.

Hither had come the scientists, engineers, social workers, mathematicians—the whole living, breathing network of mentalities responsible for cohesion in this despot-controlled world of the twenty-fourth century.

Bruce Lanning arrived late. The aerobus ways had been choked with craft all heading to the centre of Governopolis. He pushed his way in at last between the mighty black doors, and his permit gave him immediate admission to his reserved seat. Astronomer Lanning was a valued member of the Governopolis Council...and Drayton Konda, the Master, knew it well. Perhaps—too well.

Lanning's sharp grey eyes went over the sea of faces white, yellow, and black. Men and women of every clime. Some rustled papers, others silent recorders for personal use; still others just sat and waited. It was the most impressive gathering Lanning had ever seen in his ten years as chief-astronomer. Some knew why the meeting had been convened. Others did not.

Lanning was one of those who did. and he had come

to make a stand. The Master dare not. A hush fell. Muttering subsided. A loudspeaker in the black cupola of roof gave forth the harsh, impartial announcement so often heard throughout the world—

"Silence for the Master! Silence for He Who Rules!"

Automatically opened doors back of the immense rostrum permitted a figure to appear. There was not a soul in the Solar System who did not recognise him— massive, well over six feet, ox-shouldered, heavy-necked, with a truly remarkable and altogether round bald head. His brow went up in a straight line, curved over the top of his hairless skull, then went down in a straight line at the back. Intellectual, unsentimental, utterly stubborn.

As usual he was quietly dressed in the lounge suit of the time. In two strides he reached the main desk, flicked the microphone switch, and waited. Far over-head winked the eyes of television cameras. His image was being picked up and hurled to the furthest reaches of the cosmos.... Bruce Lanning smiled a little crook-edly. Though from his position he could not see the face clearly he knew it well enough. Hook-nosed, tight-lipped, square-jawed. Eyes as blue and cold as a glacier.

Drayton Konda had set himself out to master the world and the Solar System, and what was more important, he had done it. Whether for ill or for good nobody seemed to know. Perhaps because nobody was permitted to say....

Konda spoke. His voice was hard-etched, biting, purposeful. He went straight to his subject without friendly preamble.

"I have decided we need more power! Vast power! Endless power!"

Transiently he looked about him, lips out-thrust as though he challenged denial. None came. He continued talking:

"When I gained control of Earth and the Solar System, I promised it should be for a definite purpose. It was. We cannot be confined to a mere Solar System whose boundaries end with the known planets. All the neighbour worlds and satellite colonies are under the control of Earth. Therefore, I shall reach further. Outward to Alpha Centauri; then to the furthest stars! But here on Earth there is not enough power for the construction of interstellar ships; not enough power to feed endless chains of factories. We have atomic force and we have the natural power of Earth itself generated at the north magnetic pole, but more is needed! More! There remains one powerhouse still to be tapped, the greatest of them all. The *sun*!"

There was a murmur and then silence. Lanning's eyes narrowed. Now it was coming, just as he had expected.

Konda continued: "My solar engineers inform me that it is possible to erect a vast powerhouse for the sole purpose of utilising the sun's surplus power. We all know that the vast percentage of the sun's power is wasted. Drawn to a focus by magnetism it can be used, transformed to feed our chains of factories. Our output can be tripled. In five years we shall be ready to launch the greatest attempt to conquer the Universe within the history of Mankind. War? No, conquest! For this purpose of erecting a giant magnetic power plant I have convened this meeting, so that you can make the depositions for the necessary labour.

"Engineers, you will submit plans for the intended powerhouse. Labour chiefs, you will estimate the labour required. Social workers, you will broadcast statements on the benefits that can accrue. Mathematicians, you will determine the calculations. Astronomers, you will determine the effects of this process—"

"That I have already done!"

Bruce Lanning had jumped up, his voice cutting across the Master's and echoing through the hall's vast reaches. There was a dumbfounded silence. That anybody should dare to interrupt He Who Rules....

Then the automatic analyser gave forth a harsh announcement: "The interrupter is Bruce Lanning. First Astronomer to the Council of Governopolis. Guards, remove him!"

"Remove me if you will," Lanning said, standing his ground, "but I am determined that certain facts shall be known—"

"You have dared to interrupt He Who Rules," stated the Voice.

"And I will again, if it be in the common interest!"

Gathering uproar, amazement, a desperate pulling at Lanning's coat tails by his nearest neighbours—then the Master spoke.

"You may speak, Astronomer Lanning, provided it

is in the interests of Governopolis. Continue."

"I submit, sir, that your scheme for harnessing solar power will bring more destruction than benefit. In my position as Astronomer to the Council I have known for some time of your intention to utilise the sun's surplus power. Your scheme, as I see it, involves a system of magnetism between Earth and sun, by which process you intend to draw—as indeed Earth itself draws already in a more diffuse form—the electrons and energy streams which would otherwise scatter in space. This vast surplus you intend to convert in your powerhouse, and so supply your chains of lesser normal powerhouses...."

"You are correct," the Master conceded.

"Do that," Lanning stated deliberately, "and you will destroy the world! Firstly, your magnetism system will not only draw electronic streams, but also the brickbats and flying fragments forever hurtling through space. On this planet there will descend an incessant bombardment of incendiary material. Fires will break out. Hundreds of thousands of people will be killed. The extra amount of power gained will be counterbalanced by losses in labour and material."

Silence. And the Master meditated.

"That will not be all," Lanning added. "It is a well-known fact that electrical storms and radio interference are brought about entirely by electronic activity from the sun, worse at some periods than others. Increase the stream of electronic energy, and the whole world will be blanketed by radio static. Storms beyond imagination will lash the Earth. There are limits, sir, beyond which a man may not go."

Lanning remained silent, strained, and white-faced. The battering, watchful thousands of eyes was a vast ordeal. Then at last the Master spoke again.

"Your statement has been interesting, Astronomer Lanning, in spite of its variance from truth. You have overlooked that all the cities of the world, and Governopolis in particular, are fire- and invasion-proof. We need fear no attack from weapons of war: therefore even less need we fear a pseudo-invasion in the form of brickbats and meteorites. Storms are possible, but of trifling consequence. Radio we can control by static eliminators. Taken by and large, Astronomer Lanning, your statement may be summed up as a reactionary attempt to disturb this meeting."

Konda turned his head slightly. "You are ordered to strike out Astronomer Lanning's statements; No summary of them is to be published or transmitted. And, Lanning"—the bald head turned—"you will report to my office immediately after this meeting."

"But, sir, I—"

"Leave us!" Konda ordered.

"Astronomer Lanning, you are commanded to leave!" thundered the loudspeaker. "Guards, open the doors...."

Lanning's shoulders drooped. He knew—yes, and Drayton Konda knew too—that he was right. But if one man rules, and that man is determined to have extra power no matter what the cost....

Lanning went out through the assembly without uttering another word. The black doors closed soundlessly behind him.

* * * * * * *

On the colonnaded terrace outside the doors there was a scattering of people, mainly radio, television and press representatives. Gloomily Lanning glanced at them, then he wandered to the balcony and gazed out over the city from this high elevation.

Preposterous city, Governopolis! Mile-high towers of black ebonoid metal, lacy bridges, beacon towers, the streets incredibly distant below and picked out like serpents of smooth flickerless light. The quiet of the summer evening was upon Governopolis. There was no sound save the lazy hum of eternal power. The stars sprinkled the serene, purple heavens. Far away, the Earth-Mars space liner nosed silently to rest. Peaceful. A Paradise.

No, a mask! A mask for subdued humanity under the heel of omnipotent science. Science in the hands of a man convinced of his own godlike power, a man to whom human pity and kindness were unknown.

"And so shall this insubstantial pageant fade...," Lanning murmured, contemplating the crazy expanse.

"...and leave not a wrack behind," whispered a soft voice close to his ear.

Lanning turned abruptly, gazing into the eyes of a slender woman in a light, Grecian-style gown. Her eyes were brown and warm, eyes that still had not become clouded by the heel of oppression. The soft wind blew back the chestnut hair from a serene, oval face.

"Eleanor dearest, whatever are you doing here?" Lanning caught at her slim hands. "You know the wives of delegates are not really allowed...."

"No?" Her gaze slanted down the file of waiting people. "There are women there—wives too. *They* wait."

"But they are the wives of the Council members. I am only an astronomer—"

"The First—and the greatest in the world," Eleanor said gently. "Konda or no Konda, that is the truth."

"Take care what you say about Konda, dearest. The city is worm-eaten with pick-up cells. One word against him and—"

"Did you say your piece?" the girl interrupted. quietly.

"Oh yes, I said it." Lanning's jaw tightened. "I was told to get out."

"I expected that. But you are so right, Bruce. If Konda dares to go ahead—"

"Hush, dearest, hush!" Lanning laid a finger on her lips. "If such words as yours were ever to reach him, it would be the end."

"I wonder...would that matter so much?"

Lanning was silent for a moment, then: "As long as we still have each other, and I have a moderately good position, we can perhaps make out. At least we can hope for better things even if they never come...."

Lanning paused as the black doors of the hall swung

wide open and the delegates began to emerge with sombre faces. Lanning moved to the nearest one and caught at his arm.

"What was the final decision?" he asked quickly.

"As we expected," the man shrugged. "The power of the sun will be harnessed at the earliest moment."

The man went on his way; and on each man and woman who passed there was the brand of the Master. It was maddening. Inevitable. Lanning turned away at last and caught Eleanor's arm.

"I have to see the Master, dearest. His orders."

Eleanor nodded silent assent and Lanning hurried off. He pushed his way through the crowd along the galleries, through the immense ebonoid tunnel which linked up the buildings, up a gently rising staircase, and so at last to the mighty sealed doors behind which lay the sacrosanct territory of the Master of the System....

Lanning waited whilst a miscellany of instruments identified him, checked for weapons, registered him— then the three invincible doors opened one by one, and he was in Konda's presence. Slowly he walked to the massive desk and waited.

Konda's bald head was a white patch where the desk light shone upon it. The remainder of the great office was thickly shadowed. Then he looked up suddenly and the white patch was replaced with the friendless, glacier-blue eyes.

"What I have to say will not take long, Astronomer Lanning. You are suspended from duty for a period of eight weeks."

Lanning stared. "What! Just because I stated truths at—"

"What you said, was calculated to cast a reflection on my knowledge, and that I cannot allow. It was finally decided that the powerhouse for solar energy shall be erected immediately. And if you remain in your position, it will be believed that I am in secret agreement with you. Therefore, for the period of time occupied in building the powerhouse—eight weeks—you will be absent."

"But, sir, in a city like this, without work— It means starvation!" Lanning clutched at the edge of the desk. "You are taking away my only means of livelihood. You are tearing up my privilege-ticket for food, my voucher for money, my permit as an honoured Council member—"

"You should have thought of these possibilities before you dared to question my judgment at the meeting. You may go."

Lanning turned bemusedly, backing towards the huge door. Half-aware, he heard the buzz of the Master's desk phone. Then suddenly:

"Lanning!"

Lanning looked up eagerly and marched back to the desk. But there was no sign of recant in those pale blue eyes.

"Lanning, you and your wife discussed matters beyond your province on the colonnade tonight. That was most unwise."

Lanning's face tautened. "It was nothing important—"

"I know exactly what you said, and your wife too. The electronic ear recorded every word of it. I have just heard it from headquarters. I gather that I am drunk with power, that you are right and I am wrong. Your wife spoke very unwisely, Lanning."

"Look, Konda, if you even dare to touch her I'll—"

Lanning stopped dead, gulping down his surging fury as the black shadows suddenly sprouted with the grim muzzles of ray guns. He remembered. Robot guards, controlled from the desk. They were everywhere, all over the city, prying, peeping, protecting the baleful genius who was Master of the System.

"Sit down!" Konda commanded, and then snapped a switch. "Find Eleanor Lanning and bring her here immediately."

During the leaden silence that followed there was no sound save the scratch of the Master's pen as he went on with his work. Lanning sat and sweated, inwardly scalded with murderous fury. There was a click and a concealed door opened. A man in black entered, a man with a pick-axe face, dark, shrunken eyes, and pinched forehead.

Melicot! The most hated man in the System outside Konda, a legal wizard in whose hands rested the absolute enforcement of law. All infractions, however small, were examined by Melicot with ruthless thoroughness.

He sat down beside Konda and relaxed, his mouth a thin scratch and the rest of his face in shadow. Then Eleanor came in by the main doorway, calmly showing no trace of fear, though she must have known that only an ominous reason could have needed her presence here. The city guards released her.

"Eleanor!" Lanning leapt up and seized her hand.

She smiled—that slow, confident smile. Then the Master spoke.

"Eleanor Lanning, I understand you disapprove of my leadership?"

"Entirely!" Eleanor faced Konda steadily.

"Eleanor!"

"The Master asked my opinion, and I have given it," Eleanor said simply. "In fact, Konda, I loathe everything you stand for. There will come a day when—"

"Be silent," Konda interrupted. He snapped a switch, and the conversation on the terrace was played back into the shadowy gloom.

"Yes, I said all that," Eleanor admitted, when it was over.

"You realise just how much you have broken the law?"

Eleanor nodded. "Yes, I do. But I would sooner die a speaker of truth than live a liar. If there were only one man or woman with character and courage in this despot-crushed world, you would no longer rule millions from this desk."

"Eleanor!" Bruce Lanning groaned.

"I mean that for you too, Bruce," she said, turning. "It is said that one cannot overthrow this dictatorship. One man can because one man became dictator. If it comes to a choice of characters, the Master is the stronger because he got what he set out for. Somewhere, someday, there must rise one strong enough to break him—"

Melicot's acid voice broke in: "Schedule 19, Ruling 22. Anybody who speaks in condemnation of the supreme authority exercised by He Who Rules shall suffer the full penalty of the law. The penalty is death."

Konda stood up. "You have heard the sentence, Eleanor Lanning. It will be exacted at dawn tomorrow." He motioned the guards.

"You can't do it!" Lanning screamed. "You can't condemn my wife like that, just to satisfy your damned, stinking laws! I'll break you for this, Konda! I'll tear the blasted city in pieces to get you—"

"Bruce...." It was Eleanor's quiet voice. She laid a hand on his arm. Konda did not stop her. Deep down in his cast-iron soul there was a vague admiration for her serenity.

"Bruce, I knew after what I said that it would be the end. But I would rather die than live any longer in the hell that Konda has made of this world. Even Konda cannot forever separate us. I'll be waiting for you."

"No! No!" Lanning flung out a protecting arm but the blow of a guard sent him reeling back. Dazed, he shook himself, watching as the girl was led from the office. Then, like a tiger, he swung back on Konda. Melicot had already melted into the shadows.

"I'm going to stop this, Konda! My wife shall not die! You hear? You can't get away with it! Just because her opinion doesn't happen to conform to regulations!"

Konda gazed like a snake. "Eight weeks' suspension, Astronomer Lanning, then you can return to your post. You tried to prevent your wife's foolish utterances whilst on the terrace, and that weighs in your favour. Your life shall be spared. You may go."

"You bet I'll go! And I'll give you all-fired hell before I'm through!"

Lanning went, but with, the deep inner consciousness of having spoken useless words. Konda was supreme.

* * * * * * *

Cooling from anger, grief descended upon Lanning. Grief and helpless fury. He wandered the pedestrianways instead of going back to the apartment. And he knew that all the time he was watched. Sometimes the watcher was human; at other times he could sense the faint static bristling through his scalp which denoted a television beam fixed upon him from headquarters—watching and recording every move.

Once he pondered committing suicide as he gazed down from the mile-high ramparts into the bowls of light below. But where would be the good of that? Before he could have fallen any distance automatic nets would have thrust out from the building face to save him. Suicides were almost unknown in Governopolis. Konda took good care of his workers. He needed them. Surgery, too, could rapidly put things right in the case of a self-inflicted injury....

So Lanning wandered again, stunned nearly into

amnesia by the tragedy that had descended upon him. Every time he paused he found he was in a different part of the city and not quite sure how he had got there. As before, his wanderings were not interfered with. As long as he made no attempt to end his life he was safe. Safe! What a mockery!

And each time he paused he seemed to see one of the giant city clocks slicing off more of the night hours. Slowly the summer dawn began to creep over the eternally wakeful city, and he was drawn by an irresistible impulse to the vast grey façade of the city prison—there to wait, dispirited and hag-ridden, outside the walls.

Upon the stroke of four a.m. he saw the telltale light signal wink and expire on the prison roof, the sole announcement to the unheeding millions that one of their number was dead.

"Eleanor...," Lanning whispered, his eyes unashamedly blurred with tears. "Eleanor...!"

The City, merciless and unfeeling. absorbed Bruce Lanning into its matrix thereafter. It assimilated him completely, threw him out afterwards as indigestible, branded its brutal machine-stamp upon him as he moved from place to place in a half-waking nightmare. Deprived of his work, without any amenities, he became one of the drifters that must always lie back of a titanic monster of power like Governopolis.

He did not know why he tried to keep himself alive—and yet he did. Without realising it he drifted down to the lowest regions where the scum of outcast workers survived, those for whom the City no longer had any use and who were left to starve or die as circumstance dictated. Konda had his reasons for this. too. To let them rot and starve there just beyond the City was a good example to other workers if they ever thought of rebellion. Even enslavement was better than the pitiless struggle waged against death in the dark sombre alleys of the City's backwaters.

Then one night light came back into Lanning's hammered brain. It was rekindled by a few words from the man who had trailed around with him in the past weeks—a shoddy, old, bitter man with cavernous eyes and a consumptive cough.

"They finished the solar power plant today, Lanning."

"They—finished—the—plant?" Lanning said the words haltingly "Finished the—" He stopped. The words had sunk in. It suddenly linked him up with the past. The solar power plant! Eleanor!

"How long did it take?" he asked deliberately

"Eight weeks, but it's finished."

Lanning looked down at his hands, as though he had never seen them before. He inspected his torn and ragged clothing felt at his bristling stubble.

"Crawford," he said at length, "my punishment is over. I am entitled to go back there— There!" He jerked his head to the infinite blaze of light and power. "I was suspended."

"I know. I heard." Crawford coughed sepulchrally. "You can go back, take orders, and do as you're damn well told."

"But at least I can live," Lanning breathed. "Not rot in this stinking backwater. Isn't that worth something?"

Crawford spat. "I'd sooner die than work anymore for Konda. He threw me out, so I stay out. Rotting maybe, but out! And you are still willing to obey him after he had your wife executed? I just can't believe that."

"She died because she spoke the truth." Lanning got up. "Yes, because she dared to stand alone in this godless emptiness and denounce Konda to his face. There was courage, Crawford—courage such as this world hasn't seen for generations. I was not worthy of her. It was right for her to be taken away from me. But now— Now I'm changed."

"You're going to get revenge? Can't be done."

"She said that one man—" Lanning spoke half to himself. "One man—and she meant it for me. One man to free the world! Yes, Crawford, I'm going back to take up my old job, praying to God I shall not be such a coward as I once was. Then one day—"

He straightened up. "I have to get myself in order. The past died in these eight weeks of hell. For me there is only the future...."

* * * * * * *

So Lanning reported for duty again, and with the impartiality of the law his social security was restored to him. He returned to being a cog in the Council machine, but he knew he was eternally watched. The mark of suspicion was upon him—but he did nothing to nurture that suspicion.

That he had returned for vengeance there was no doubt, but to want it and achieve it were as apart as the galaxies. All he could do was wait for an opportunity and keep his mouth shut. At least he had a better chance in the Council than in being a drifter.

He made his astronomical reports with religious exactness, came and went from and to his coldly empty apartment every day, never made mistakes and never appeared rebellious. But it was noticed that he never smiled. Never.

Then, little by little, some of the things he had predicted for the solar magnetiser began to occur. At intervals there were showers of brickbats upon the city. In some parts of the world the showers were heavy enough to inflict considerable injury and damage. It then became part of his work to predict the paths of the meteor streams. When he had the prediction complete the magnetiser was switched off to allow the meteor fields to stream past unattracted.

To Lanning it simply meant that his postulations were correct. Nothing more. He had been justified in his warnings, but he was not avenged. Not yet.

Storms came next, stirred up by the onslaught of electronic streams upon the higher planes of the atmosphere. In six nights out of seven, as the heat of the summer gave way to the coolness of the autumn, there were rolling thunderstorms over monstrous Governopolis. Lightning exploded itself in random bolts at the mile-high towers with their huge insulator-caps. Rain descended in a flood from the raging, tortured heaven. The world over, radio became impossible at such times, despite the unceasing influence of the static-eliminator plants....

These were the nights that Lanning loved. Perched high in the major observatory, he was alone, the rest of the staff being isolated in other parts of the building. Here he could watch the furious blaze of the storm around the giant dome of warpless glass, could feel at one with the fury because it had something in common with his own tortured soul. On such nights as these he could imagine the spirit of Eleanor abroad. Her name now was like a timeless echo. A bold, magnificent woman who had died because she had spoken the truth.

"Truth!" Lanning whispered, his eyes fixed on the tumult. "Truth—and vengeance! A bridge between! I am that bridge!"

Lightning crackled violet fire.

"If only there were one man—!" screamed the wind.

"Konda! Konda! KONDA!" crashed the thunderbolts.

"I shall be waiting...." A faint, clear thread of remembrance.

"Vengeance!" Lanning breathed, his face wet with the fury of his emotions. "Yes, there shall be vengeance! Eleanor!" He tore the safety-window open and yelled into the wind and rain. "Eleanor, do you hear me? You shall be avenged. I am the bridge!"

Then he turned away, cold and calm, and fastened the window. These moods were common now. Perhaps he was half mad: he did not know. And slowly the storm began to die away. The stars winked into view. Lanning calmed then settled himself in the chair of the giant telescope to make his nightly charts.

It was quite by chance that the huge instrument was turned on the eastern heaven, and since Earth had shifted since the last observation the instrument was not trained on the previous night's field but upon the orbit of Nemesis, the massive meteorite-comet which made a round trip in something like seventy-seven years. First appearing at the beginning of the previous century, having been somehow diverted from the outer deeps of the Solar System, it had pursued its journey regularly, always coming near to but never touching Earth.

But this time! Lanning stared, and stared. The sweeping tail of Nemesis was different. It was fore-shortened, and it had never been foreshortened before.

Lanning found his hand trembling on the controls. This meant something big. Suddenly he deserted his chair and hurried over to the files concerning the visitor. Hurriedly, tensely, he waded through spectro-heliographs, plates, mathematical computations. No doubt about it! Nemesis was off course! But why? What cosmic accident had caused this thing?

Back of his mind Lanning knew what had caused it, but he did not dare just then to give his imagination free rein. It seemed impossible that Fate had given him such a supreme chance to prove himself right.

All that night he remained at the telescope, spent the next day making calculations; then when the next night came—clear and calm for a change—he went to work again. Swinging the giant instrument to where the comet should appear, if following its normal orbit, he found no trace of it! Tensely, he swung back to the position of the previous night. Nemesis was still there, a trifle larger, deep yellow in colour, and the tail had gone.

Stunned. Lanning stared at the unbelievable. It could only mean one thing. Nemesis had turned right off her course and the tail was now invisible because it was streaming right out behind her and could not be seen from Earth. Nemesis was hurtling towards Earth from outer space, inexorably drawn, and there was a reason for that, too.

With the dispassionate calm of the true astronomer, shelving for the time his personal hates and bitterness, Lanning went to work. When he had all his notes complete—and it took him a week, during which time Nemesis had grown enormously—he gathered them up and left the observatory.

Dawn had just broken. He took the quiet routes that led to Drayton Konda's headquarters. The Master always reached his desk at dawn, and had just arrived when Lanning was shown in to him.

"Well, Astronomer Lanning?"

If the Master was surprised at the early call he did not show it, but his steely eyes had curiosity in them.

Lanning said briefly: "When you first erected the solar power plant, sir, I warned you of danger. You refused to listen. I forecast the doom of the world. That doom—is coming!"

Konda's face was expressionless. "Explain yourself."

"A meteorite-comet, Nemesis by name, has been swung aside from her normal path of seventy-seven years circuit. The reason for that is the immense force field generated by your power station reaching out into space. You are using magnetism. This meteorite has a large percentage of magnetic oxide of iron, instantly drawn by magnetism, far more so than by gravitation, which is not magnetism. It has been caught in the field of your magnet and is heading straight for Earth. Its speed is seven thousand miles a minute: its size, half that of the moon. Its gas envelope is highly poisonous. Here are the official records."

Konda took them, studied them, then tightened his lips.

"I will give orders for the power station to be cut off instantly and so free this thing whilst it is still far away."

"That will avail exactly nothing!" Lanning smiled icily. "It is in a fixed path now and on the opposite side from the sun. It is making a beeline for Earth and nothing can stop it hitting us. The damage is done!"

"We could go underground," Konda mused. "That way we could withstand the impact."

"Its speed, when it reaches here, will be in the region

of eight thousand miles a second," Lanning stated. "You have eight days in which to get below—no more. Even if you could do it, it wouldn't save you. I warned you, Konda, that too much power would break you one day. Now it's my turn! I shall tell the people of the world what your blind ambition has brought upon them! The end of the world! Some of them may still be able to escape to another planet."

"I think not," Konda said slowly. "The people shall know nothing of this. That you have come to me first with the information saves the situation. They shall know nothing!"

"You can't do it, Konda! When the comet becomes visible in the next night or two explanations will be demanded from you, the Master!"

"And if the Master is not here?" Konda asked softly.

"What?" Lanning stared at him. "You can't mean— you're going to desert Earth?"

"My life is more valuable than that of the worker. If this planet is doomed, I shall move to one that is not. I have the mastery of every planet in the System—don't forget that. I owe you a debt, Astronomer Lanning, for bringing this matter to my notice."

"So you'll make good your escape and leave the millions who've sweated and died for you? This is one time you won't get away with it—"

"Lanning, you're becoming a nuisance," Konda said, a ray gun suddenly in his hand. "It is time to be rid of you, but not in a way that anybody can know what happened to you. If inquiry is made, you have simply become deranged and been removed. I shall withdraw all other astronomers from duty before the threat of Nemesis can be fully ascertained. I shall not even entrust you to an executioner, because he may talk. You shall go into space, amongst those beloved stars of yours—to die!"

"Now wait a minute!" Lanning snapped. "All right, I'm half mad. I want revenge for the death of my wife—all right again. But duty to humanity comes first. There may yet be a way to avert this catastrophe. Fleets of space machines firing neutron guns could perhaps explode this comet before it strikes us—its metallic core, anyway. The gas we would have to provide against. Or you might arrange counter-attractors on other planets to draw it aside and neutralise its danger. There are many things—"

"You said eight days, Lanning. There is not the time. Besides, I have never considered it wise to trifle with the cosmos. If I cannot be certain of beating it I allow it full play."

Konda got up suddenly. "Walk!" he commanded. "It is a favourable moment for your departure, before the staff gets here. Walk!"

Lanning clenched his fists, wondering which was best—space-death as Konda had planned for him, or the sudden death of the flame-gun. Finally he walked. Life is not an easy thing to sell as long as there is a spark of hope left....

With the gun in his back he walked the still deserted galleries in the fresh morning air, ascended the spiral stairway, and finally reached the private spacedrome on top of the executive building. Konda motioned him to a one-man flyer. He climbed in and sat down in the control chair. Before he realised what had happened manacles snapped into position around wrists and ankles. He raised a startled face.

"You were prepared for this then, Konda?"

"No. But there have been others whom it was necessary to be rid of in the same quiet way as this. This ship is specially constructed for undesirables...."

He leaned over the switchboard and made adjustments to the complicated mechanism, checked the fuel gauge, then turned an expressionless face.

"The time-switch mechanism is set to start in five minutes," he said. "It will operate, hurtle the ship well clear of Earth, and will then send it on a straight-line journey. You will travel clear out of the Solar System, will keep on going until the power fails. By then you will be beyond Pluto and will maintain a constant velocity until some cosmic body attracts the ship. If by then you have not starved, you will die, ground to powder, and no man will ever know."

Lanning could not think of anything to say. The merciless workings of Konda's mind were beyond his gauging. First it had been Eleanor, because she had spoken the truth. Now it was himself, for exactly the same reason. And he had thought he had found a perfect lever to bring Konda's kingdom crashing—!

The airlock clicked shut. Lanning stared bleakly at the control board, striving without avail to break the grip of the manacles. He waited through the longest five minutes he had ever known.

Suddenly the crushing pressure of the start was upon him. In his ears was the roar of the rocket jets, and through the ports he saw Earth bathed in pallid morning mist as he climbed into the infinite. Straight as an arrow, perfectly charted, the vessel hurtled into the star-pricked immensity of space

Lanning sat immovable, pinned down, but after a while a sensation of deepening alarm settled upon him as he felt a distant pull of the ship out of its charted direction

The nose was turning, slowly and inexorably, into the field of the titanic solar powerhouse magnet, a field existing between Earth and sun. Lanning found himself wondering what would happen. So far no spaceship had ever been near that deadly line. Paths had been charted to give it as wide a berth as possible...but in his urgency to be rid of his greatest enemy Konda had overlooked that this was only a small ship unprotected by giant rockets able to fire it away from the counter-pull.

The next thing he knew he was in the midst of the mystery-field. He could not analyse what was happening to him. His body was shot through with mind-numbing pain. He was alive and yet dead, caught in a fiery cramp that felt as though each nerve were exploding separately. His brain, right out of tune with his body, made him feel as though he were in two places at once, then the sensation blasted into a white-heat of anguish as his body felt as though it were bulging to breaking point. He stared at hands and arms bloated like balloons save for the narrow necks where the manacles gripped.

A ripping sensation made him scream with pain, but with it his mind returned to normal and the pain stopped. For a second or two he revelled in the sweet langour pervading him. Then he began to look around him. His hands caught his attention. Something was desperately wrong. His hands were like glass! He could see through them! Frightened, he looked down at himself. Everything that clothing did not hide was transparent!

Nor was this all, for with a sudden effort he lifted his hands clean through the manacles! Just as though his wrists were ploughing through cloying dough. Even as he got shakily to his feet he noticed he sank a little into the metal floor, finding solidity at about two inches' depth It took him a long time to master himself; then terror gave way to scientific curiosity.

Turning to the switchboard he found he had just sufficient solidity in his fingers to move the levers. He cast aside the automatic devices and gave full blast to the rear tubes. Gradually he got the ship pulling away from the magnetic beam. He waited, wondering if he would regain his normal appearance once he was back in free space. His amazement was complete when transparency remained even when clear of the magnetic beam.

Puzzled, he started to think, going back over each of

his sensations. Magnetism? Opposing forces. The truth filtered in slowly and made him gasp. The atoms of his body had coordinated! That was it.... Normally, the atoms and molecules of his body—any body—should be chasing hither and yon, the products of disorganized magnetism. Yet each atom and molecule possesses north and south poles. Magnetism. Disorganized. But if a gigantic force. a strange form of magnetism—such as that issuing from Konda's magnetic powerhouse— were to cause all those atoms to turn their poles in one direction?

"I'd become as a ghost," Lanning whispered. "Semi-transparent and able to walk through matter. The stray atoms still not turned by magnetism would make for a slight resistance. That is the 'dough' effect and the reason why I sink right through the floor. The majority of the atoms and molecules in my body have been turned in one direction, swung by the magnetism from Konda's power plant. His magnetism reacts on human structure, evidently, but not on the artificially toughened matter of the ship."

This puzzled him for a moment, but when he came to look closely, he saw that the vessel had also suffered a slight transparency.

"And nothing can put me right except demagnetisation," Lanning mused. "Any more than an ordinary magnet can lose its magnetism without special treatment."

Slowly the possibilities began to dawn upon him. He was unkillable, changed by the scientific fluke into a man to whom matter was no barrier, to whom a bullet meant no danger, to whom a death ray meant no more than a flash of light. Vengeance was his to exact at last! There remained—Konda! He had said he would escape to another world. Good! Lanning smiled icily. He would wait for him.

But two days and nights passed without any sign of spaceships leaving Earth. The reason was fairly obvious. The perturbations from onrushing Nemesis were making space itself like a stormy sea. Lanning could feel his own vessel rocking constantly. Time was moving fast. The comet had grown hugely in forty-eight hours.... So Lanning went back to Earth. The moment he was in the atmosphere he was amidst hot vapours, the view hidden in a smoky haze of dust brought about by the meteoric matter streaming ahead of the comet-meteorite itself. At intervals Lanning caught glimpses of men and women coming and going.

He landed at the space port amidst a fiery gloom. Eventually he beheld a spaceport official in the murk and caught hold of him. The man's eyes stared as though they would drop out.

"Bruce Lanning!" he whispered. "The ghost of Bruce Lanning!"

"Where is Konda?" Lanning demanded.

"Nobody knows. The people got wise to this approaching asteroid and demanded Konda should protect them. He said he couldn't. He fled into the city somewhere—"

Lanning was on his way, striding into the smoke.

He went first to the main centre of the city. Heat-haze was everywhere. Moving, terrified people were too concerned with themselves to notice this hazy ghost of a man who sought revenge. Lanning went on, across bridges, through walls, through sealed doors. On and on until the night fell. Here Lanning paused, took what food he could find—for he still needed it—rested, and then set to again. Night was baleful in its terror. Nemesis was fully visible through the heat-fog, filling half the heavens, rolling and swelling and pouring its insufferable warmth down on the world. So suddenly had it appeared, so completely had Konda suppressed all news of it, there was no time left to avoid it. Four days and nights maybe, then—

Lanning's jaw tightened. Something like ninety-six hours left in which to find Konda.

Night—and day again. Night again. Day again. Night— And still he searched, and ate, and rested. The heavens were a mass of orange light; the sky a vortex. His endless searching took him through buildings in which were huddles of people praying for deliverance....

The heavens changed to flaming scum. In two hours maybe the atmosphere would ignite. Life would vanish like tinder in a furnace. So Lanning came at last to the great solar powerhouse. Its engines were quiet and the staff had gone. But there was one lone figure with a bald head. Lanning smiled and walked down the main aisleway. Presently Konda caught sight of him and stared in frozen horror.

"How'd—how'd you get here?" he whispered. "You're a ghost!"

"Does that matter?" Lanning demanded. "In a matter of minutes Nemesis will hit Earth. Our atmosphere will go. Tons of liquid rock will crash down into this powerhouse. Only space could have saved you, and you couldn't get away from the mob. Millions will, die because of you, but at this moment I'm thinking of my wife who died because she told the truth. Damn you, Konda—damn you!"

Lanning's semi-transparent hands flashed out, seizing Konda's powerful neck. The fingers sunk further than normal, but at last they found resistance. They crushed, harder and harder, until Konda sank to his knees.

"Lanning!" he choked desperately. "Lanning, a chance!"

Lanning gave no answer. He screwed his fingers until he felt them crack. A faint smile curved his lips as he saw the purpling face and starting eyes....

Suddenly it came. The powerhouse shook. Heat rolled suddenly through the place, as though it had been dipped in molten lead. Walls, floor, ceiling, machines—all began to liquefy. Flames caught the dead Konda's clothes and set them blazing. Lanning, too, felt the insufferable anguish of heat as the atoms and molecules of his body began to regain their normal haphazard positions under the influence of rising temperature. But to what end?

Hotter—and hotter. He felt himself melting away.

But across the tumult of a dying world, there came a faint clear echo.

"I shall be waiting...."

"Leave—not—a—wrack—behind," Lanning found himself thinking, and the inhuman truth of it blazed across his dying brain.

THREE'S A CROWD

The hour of glory was over, but nevertheless it had been of such an order as to make it unforgettable. The first expedition to an unexplored region of South America had returned intact, bringing with it one more member than had gone on the outward journey—the exquisite Verona, daughter of the ruler of the lost tribe that the explorers had discovered. What made matters all the more astonishing was that her peoples were far from being primitive savages, but had—for reasons that were still being investigated—elected to cut themselves off from civilization for centuries. To her there was now wedded Bruce Langden, leader of the expedition which had discovered her domain, under the expert navigation of Captain Jack Anderson.

Yes, the day of the anthropological world's acclaim, the curiosity of the media, the interviews and nights of banqueting, were finished. Langden, Captain Anderson, and indeed every member of the expedition, were wealthy for life, mainly from the books they had yet to write upon their discoveries. The real story about the mysterious lost tribe was eagerly awaited by the world—were they really descendants of the long-vanished Incas?

But Bruce Langden was in no hurry to answer the questions. Months of strain and travel had given way now to sweet relaxation, relaxation with Verona at the villa Langden had bought for their honeymoon in the south of France. Here, in the hot sunlight of summer's height, he and Verona were gradually working out for themselves the pattern of the future.

Yes, Verona was a very beautiful woman, golden-brown skinned like the rest of her race, differing in no way from the normal physical standards attributed to a woman of equatorial South America. Her hair was intensely black, her features regular, and her mouth small. She was tallish in stature and moved with the majestic grace that was her heritage, descended from the ruling clique of her people. Highly intelligent, her ability to learn and master the English language so quickly had been astonishing.

"To me, Bruce dearest," Verona murmured one evening as they sat in the twilight of your terrace, "everything about your western world seems so orderly, so very—er—self-possessed. It reminds me of a big house, perfectly kept, whereas my own world had everything higgledy-piggledy."

Bruce laughed. For one thing Verona's newly acquired English was spoken in delightful halts and lisps; and for another her smiles were more than quaint.

"Big house or not, my dear, it's yours and mine." Bruce put his arm about her slender shoulders and drew her to him.

"Yes...." Verona gazed absently at the darkening western sky. "Sometimes, though, I become afraid when I think of how much I have yet to learn—about your people, your customs. Your civilization is much ahead of ours."

"Just the luck of things," Bruce murmured. "We have been able to advance our scientific knowledge because our different cultures came together and pooled their discoveries. We've even mastered space travel, amongst other things! And medical science can treat almost all known diseases.... Your people seem to have remained isolated for centuries, and so missed out...."

"Which knowledge you are prepared to give to my people?"

"Well—er—it's not mine to give, Verona. It belongs to our world governments, and it is for them to give the permission. I am quite sure they will. But those deeper commercial issues are not our concern. The future belongs to us."

Verona was silent. A faint, warm breeze disturbed the soft fairness of her hair. Bruce could dimly see those great eyes of hers gazing westwards. There was a certain wistful sadness about her expression.

"Homesick?" he whispered presently.

"No, it isn't that. It's—" Verona hesitated, then rose abruptly. "Let's go inside, Bruce, it's getting chilly."

"Okay. I'd forgotten you're a hothouse plant!"

Bruce followed her majestic figure across the terrace and into the lounge of the villa. He closed the French windows, switched on the standard lamp, and looked at Verona intently. The little lines of sadness were still there, but it struck him they had taken on an edge of anxiety too.

"What *is* it, dearest?" he asked in concern, going over to her. "Whatever your problem may be, I'm here to help you. I know you must find it difficult to fit yourself into the pattern of a different world, so—"

"It isn't that. Bruce. I can't explain it. It's something entirely personal."

"Oh—I see." Bruce stood awkwardly. "I'm sorry."

"There's nothing to be sorry about," Verona smiled. "In some things we differ, Bruce dearest—that's inevitable with our opposite heritages. If I ever seem moody, don't worry about it—it's just a part of me."

"I'll remember that." Bruce tried to show unconcern by moving needlessly around the lounge. "Matter of fact, I think this place stuck here in southern France is too quiet for both of us. You need the surroundings of London, and I'm darned sure I do. More life, more gaiety altogether. The others who were with us on the expedition can easily pop in when they want and liven things up. Good old Jack Anderson and the rest of them. Eh?"

Verona nodded absently as she settled slowly on the divan.

"Yes, perhaps that would help.... After all, I cannot get to know your people really well unless I mix with them can I?"

"Of course not!" Bruce, big and clumsy, threw

himself down on the divan beside her. With unmeaning roughness he drew her head down towards his shoulders. "The more you mix with them, the happier you'll be. I'm wondering, though, if I'm not sticking my neck out by having Jack Anderson drop in whenever he wants. He and I ran it pretty close in our devotion for you."

Verona smiled. "I married you, didn't I? How much more convincing proof do you want?"

* * * * * * *

Bruce did not waste any time. Within a week he had completed his negotiations for a city home—one of the most modern residences in London, and to here he and Verona moved at the earliest opportunity. Even so, there was still something wrong. Bruce could sense it, and it upset his blunt, forthright nature that he could not immediately pinpoint the trouble. Back of everything he was haunted by the dismal fear that perhaps Verona had grown tired of him. After all, they belonged to different cultures. Was this perhaps an irreconcilable problem?

It became more and more obvious as time passed that the change to city life was not the answer to Verona's moodiness. The constant coming and going of friends—particularly big Jack Anderson, who never seemed to tire of Verona's company—did not produce much change in the golden-skinned girl. Rather there was the opposite effect, and she began to make excuses to avoid meeting people. Upon which Bruce did the only thing he could. He shut the doors on everybody—at least until he had got to the root of the riddle in his wife's outlook.

"At least give me some reasonable explanation," he insisted on the first quiet evening he and Verona were able to have together. "I don't know whether it's good form in your society to sit around looking sullen, but it certainly isn't the thing here!"

Verona gave a brief glance of reproach from her extraordinary eyes, and immediately Bruce felt willing to kick himself.

"Sorry, Verry. I didn't mean that—I'm just wondering what to do next to try and make you happier. If you're ill; if you find our climate a burden to you—though I can't think why you should since there's not all that much difference—then say so. I'll see what can be done to have our specialists put you right."

"I'd be better—a whole lot better—if I were left entirely to myself for about two weeks."

"Eh?" Bruce said unbelievingly, "But—but I thought you said that you couldn't get to know my people really well unless you mixed with them. Now you want to be left alone!"

"I do. I'm weighed down with a psychological condition, an aspect of the mind, far too complicated to explain. I'm quite sure it has been caused by my being uprooted from my home. Give me two weeks to commune with myself and I'll be all right—for all time to come. You see—" Verona's slim hand moved as she caught at the right phrase. "It's a matter of adjustment."

"And I'm in the way!"

"You're never that, dearest. Please try to understand."

"God knows, I'm trying to, but— Oh well, all right." Bruce gave a shrug. "I don't pretend to be able to understand the mind of a woman, Just as long as you put yourself right, I don't mind what happens. Come to think of it, I've quite a bit of unfinished business to attend to up in Scotland concerning the expedition. Suppose I go and attend to it and leave you alone. That suit?"

For once an eager brightness came into Verona's eyes. Bruce did not know whether he approved of it or not.

"That would solve everything, Bruce! You do that, and when you come back I'll have all the snarls in my mind straightened out."

"Okay, but—I don't altogether like leaving you alone except for the servants, that is. Shall I have some of the gang look in on you from time to time? Jack Anderson and some of the girls, maybe—?"

"No, Bruce! No! You can't straighten out a mental upheaval when others are around. I'll be all right with just the servants."

Which had to suffice. Bruce made the necessary arrangements and. the following day, departed for Scotland. Deliberately, he made no contact with home, in any form whatever. He felt vaguely peeved when Verona did not contact him either, but mollified himself with the thought that she was sticking to her intention to preserve splendid isolation.

By and large, he was thankful when the fortnight was up, and wasted no time getting home. To his inner joy he found a radiant Verona awaiting him, a girl looking so happy a carefree it was somehow impossible to associate her memory with the moody almost estranged creature he had left behind.

"Better, darling?" Bruce asked, sweeping her up in his big arms.

"Completely, dearest!" Her feet kicked gently against his shins. "Everything that was worrying me has evaporated. I'm acclimatised now. I'm the laughing Verona you married."

Bruce set her down and looked at her seriously. "That's wonderful! I've been fretting myself to pieces in this past fortnight, wondering how you were getting on."

"Well—" She gave her pert smile. "Now you have to worry no more."

She wandered across to the settee and settled herself. Bruce followed her up after a moment and sat down beside her.

"Anybody come whilst I was away?" he asked. "Any of the original expedition, to keep you company?"

"No.... As I told you, I wanted to be alone."

"Uh-huh." Bruce accepted the answer calmly enough, but he had the curious, niggling suspicion at the back of his mind that Verona was not entirely speaking the truth. He could imagine why he should think such a thing. Perhaps he was abnormally jealous of her. Yes, that might be it. The very thought of any other man claiming her attention in the merest degree was too much for him.

"And you?" Verona asked. "How did things go up in Scotland?"

"Oh, so-so. It wasn't anything important anyway."

"I'm interested just the same."

So the conversation drifted into irrelevancies, and all the time Bruce kept thinking how incredibly changed Verona was. She was the very essence of life and vitality, her entire personality sparkling like champagne. The process of her acclimatisation to Western ways seemed indeed to be complete.

Then came the evening meal, over which the conversation still continued, until it was interrupted by a phone call. Hudson, the manservant, entered the dining room with grave calm.

"Captain Anderson is calling on the line, sir...." He glanced at Bruce. "Are you at home?"

"You bet I am," Bruce grinned, getting up. "Thanks, Hudson."

He hurried out into the hall and picked up the instruments. "Hello there, Jack! How's tricks?"

"Might ask you the same question," came Jack Anderson s matter-of-fact voice. "I've been trying to talk to you, or your wife, for the past fortnight. I was beginning to wonder where you'd both gone to."

"Past fortnight?" Bruce repeated, surprised. "I don't quite understand that. Verry's been here even though I've been up in Scotland. Anyway, skip that. Why the ring? Anything on your mind?"

"Nothing particular. I simply wondered how long it was going to be before we have another of our get-togethers? Last time we met, you shut the doors on everybody because Verry wasn't feeling too good. Doesn't have to stay that way, does it?"

"Not anymore," Bruce laughed. "She's completely got over all that and sorted herself out, particularly during the last fortnight."

"Good! When do we all meet again, then? I need hardly tell you that I'm more than anxious to see Verry again."

"Yes, I've little doubt of that," Bruce responded dryly, "But don't forget that you lost the race for her and I won it— A get-together? By all means, but I'd better see what Verry says first. Hold it over for the moment, and I'll ring you back later this evening."

"Fair enough! Give Verry my love."

Anderson rang off, and Bruce put the phone back slowly on to its cradle, frowning to himself. Abruptly he caught sigh of Hudson drifting across the lower end of the hall.

"Hudson—a moment."

The manservant silently approached. "Sir?"

"That was Captain Anderson on the phone, as you're aware. He tells me he has been trying to communicate either with me or Mrs. Langden for the past fortnight, without result. Is that correct?"

Hudson hesitated imperceptibly. "That is correct, sir."

"But surely you told my wife that he was on the phone?"

"I—er—was given instructions that she was not to be disturbed, sir."

Bruce looked at the manservant searchingly, and he seemed to very slightly flinch.

"You mean," Bruce said deliberately, "that you allowed Captain Anderson to keep ringing up and did not once inform the mistress?"

"I had my instructions, sir, and endeavoured to carry them out."

"I appreciate that, but it seems to me you put too literal an interpretation on the matter. My wife could never have meant that she was not to be disturbed *all* the time."

Hudson was silent, plainly ill at ease. There was relief in his hatchet-face as Bruce, with a jerk of the head, dismissed him. Then he returned into the dining room.

"Well?" Verona glanced towards him, smiling brightly. "What did Jack want?"

"Chiefly to know where you and I have been in the last fortnight. He rang up several times."

Verona shrugged. "I gave Hudson orders that I wasn't to be disturbed. Didn't matter who it was."

"I see. Suppose it had been me?" Bruce sat down again at the table.

"You would have been the exception, only I felt pretty sure you wouldn't ring."

"Jack Anderson," Bruce said deliberately, "is too

dear a friend of ours to be brushed off like that. Quite frankly, Verry, I find it hard to credit that you were brooding alone all the time."

"What else do you suppose I was doing?"

"No idea. Things just don't ring true somehow."

Verona gave a very direct look. "There are times, Bruce, when I think you have a very suspicious nature."

He smiled rather tautly. "It's not that. It's simply that I feel it's part of my duty to keep a constant eye on you. You are not well versed in our laws even yet, and I never know what you might do next."

Verona got to her feet abruptly, her eyes flashing. "Well, thanks very much! Because I choose to have a fortnight entirely to myself, you conjure up all sorts of dark notions, is that it?"

She did not wait to hear the answer to her question. Instead she stalked angrily from the room and slammed the door behind her. Bruce compressed his lips and looked moodily at his half-finished meal. Hudson, who had evidently observed Verona's swift departure, came in quietly to clear what remained of her meal. Bruce eyed him for a moment or two, then put his thoughts into words.

"Hudson, I have every respect for your integrity, and you have been an excellent servant since you came here."

"Thank you, sir. I do my utmost."

"Then tell me something. What did my wife do in the fortnight whilst I was away? Did she stay in her room all the time? Day and night?"

Hudson was silent, apparently trying to make up his mind over something.

"Out with it, man!" Bruce snapped, getting up. "I am the master of this house, remember, not my wife. You know as well as I do that she isn't used to our ways, and that demanded I keep a constant watch on her. Was she in her room throughout the fortnight?"

"No, sir." Hudson seemed relieved. "She was not even in the house."

"What!" Bruce stared blankly.

"I am rather glad you have pressed the point to an issue, sir. I dislike having to keep up a deception, because I have respect for you as a world explorer as well as being my employer, and I—"

"Come to the point, man! About my wife!"

"Well, sir, she left here two hours after you had departed for Scotland and she only returned yesterday, knowing, of course, that you would be back today. Before she left she gave me a—er—certain monetary consideration and the instruction that I was to say she was not to be disturbed."

"I—see. You have no idea where she went during that time, Hudson?"

"No idea at all, sir." Hudson waited for a moment, then the telephone again rang in the hall, and he went out. After a moment his voice broke in on Bruce's troubled thoughts.

"The *Evening Echo* would like a word with you, sir."

Evening Echo? What the devil could they want? Bruce wandered out to the phone and picked it up.

"Yes? Bruce Langden speaking."

"Oh, good evening, Mr. Langden. We'd just like an exclusive from you if we can. This is the city editor speaking."

"Exclusive? Concerning what?"

"Your private jet—the one in which you made the expedition to South America. Is there any truth in the rumour that you secretly made another flight, or isn't that for publication?"

With an effort Bruce tried to make himself think clearly.

"Secret flight? What on earth are you talking about, man? There's been no attempt to make any trips since we returned from South America, nor will there be until everything is planned out neat and tidy. Where did this rumour spring from?"

"Er—" The city editor hesitated; then: "Your plane is in the hangar where you left it after the return from South America. That right?"

"Quite right. In the city centre."

"Yes—but about a fortnight ago your plane took off from that hangar, and it returned yesterday evening. Couldn't be any mistake about either occurrence, because it was witnessed by ground crews and many members of the public. I tried in the last fortnight to get in touch with you, without success, so of course no news was printed. But since your plane came back yesterday I think it's time you satisfied public curiosity. You're a very famous man, Mr. Langden."

Bruce stood thinking, looking straight before him.

"I said you're a—"

"Yes, yes, I heard you," Bruce interrupted. "Just give me a little while—an hour maybe—and I'll ring you back. There's something I must straighten out concerning this business, but I can tell you right now that I personally had nothing to do with such a flight. I'll look into it."

"Very well, sir, I'll wait on you—but we must have some kind of answer quickly."

Bruce put the phone down and, grim-faced, hurried up the staircase and into the bedroom. Verona was seated at the broad window, gazing out into the gathered twilight. She turned briefly as Bruce entered.

"I want a word with you," he said bluntly, and dragging up a chair he sat down beside her.

"Well?" Her queer eyes with their now enormously distended pupils gazed at him dispassionately. She was now in one of those moods when he felt he did not know her, when the alien barrier between their different cultures had dropped.

"In the past fortnight the plane has been used," Bruce said deliberately. "Only the members of the expedition know the code of the hangar lock and how to control the vessel. Jack Anderson certainly didn't use the machine because he's been ringing up here. In the fortnight I was away you were not in this house. I have that information from Hudson."

Verona's lips tightened slightly, and Bruce was not slow to notice the fact.

"You left here the day I went to Scotland and returned

yesterday. I'll make one guess: you went somewhere in the plane."

Long silence. Verona stirred restlessly. That immense vitality she had seemed to possess earlier in the evening had vanished now.

"All right, I did," she admitted at last. "I hired a pilot to fly me there and back. Nothing wrong in it, is there? I'm as much a member of the expedition as the rest of you are, and I have my own money after the sale of some of my people's artefacts I brought with me."

"Certainly you are, but why couldn't you tell me? I could even have flown you myself."

"I couldn't see that it was really necessary that I should, and I didn't want to bother you."

Bruce drummed his fingers on his knees. "I suppose I'll have to put that down to ignorance of our ways. The fact remains you—or at least the plane—was seen both going and returning. No news of it has leaked out yet, which is one reason why I didn't know about it. But the press wants the facts. What am I supposed to tell them?"

Verona shrugged. "The truth, I suppose. In that time I flew to South America and back. I had to—I was so desperately homesick I couldn't stand it any longer. I couldn't see that it mattered. Had I told you beforehand what I intended doing, you'd have flown the plane, or had Jack Anderson do it. I didn't want that. I wanted to get my tangled thoughts straightened out a bit. I didn't have long to stay with my own people, of course, but it was enough to satisfy me. Then I came back."

Bruce relaxed slowly and then smiled. His arm stole about Verona's shoulders and drew her to him.

"I'm sorry, Verry," he muttered. "I'm too damned impulsive, that's what it is—and too suspicious. But it's only because I love you so much. Nothing wrong in what you did: entirely understandable. I'll tell the press it was just an experiment. Anything as long as you are contented and happy."

"I'd be happier," Verona whispered, "if we could go back to our villa in France. I know it's quiet, but—well, somehow I'd prefer it. You didn't sell it, did you?"

"No. I thought we'd need it—sometime. You're sure about this?"

Verona nodded, and Bruce remained silent. Though he was willing to do anything she wanted, he did find the thought of a return to that lonely villa inordinately depressing....

Verona did not return downstairs again that evening. Bruce finally left her, still at the window, and re-contacted the *Evening Echo*. His brief explanation that his wife had made a flying visit to assuage homesickness was taken with some disbelief by the city editor, but since that was the story, it was up to him to print it, without trimmings.

By the time he had dealt with this, Bruce discovered it was not far from midnight, so he returned upstairs—to find Verona already in bed, and apparently asleep. Before long he, too, was dozing, to awaken again abruptly in the dead of night.

Everything was deathly still with only the pale

ghost of moonlight to diffuse the shadows. He lay still for a moment or two, wondering what had awakened him—then as he turned his head it dawned on him that Verona was missing. Her twin bed next to his was empty. Instantly he was awake and struggling into his dressing gown. Scuffing into his slippers he hurried from the room and down the broad corridors of the great house, switching on the lights as he went. He did not call Verona by name for fear of awakening the domestics. This, he felt, was a matter that he alone must deal with.

Upstairs, Verona was nowhere to be found. Bruce hurried down the staircase, and the front door swinging open told its own story. He hurried out into the warmth of the summer night and looked about him anxiously, almost immediately catching sight of two dim figures a little way down the drive and apparently seated on the grass at one side of it.

"Verry!" Bruce called urgently, as he hurried forward. "Is it you, Verry?"

It was. She got to her feet slowly and, as he came nearer, Bruce could see she was still in her night attire with a robe sashed about it and her masses of dark hair flowing free. Her eyes looked enormous in the moonlight, and lent her an ethereal aspect. But there was nothing ethereal about the figure that arose beside her. With inward amazement Bruce instantly recognised the big, burly frame of Jack Anderson.

"Bet this looks pretty bad, eh?" Anderson grinned, holding out his hand.

"That's an understatement," Bruce retorted, keeping his own hand at his side. "What's the idea of this, Verry? Or don't you know it's not far from three o'clock?"

She gave that little shrug of hers. "I couldn't sleep. Too many things disturbing my mind. I heard somebody banging on the front door, so I went down to investigate, since you and the servants were asleep."

"And found Jack? At this hour?" Bruce could not keep the scorn out of his voice.

"Queer though it may seem, yes," Jack Anderson snapped. "I know it's an unconventional hour, but then I'm an unconventional fellow."

"So it seems!"

"Hear me out, can't you? You promised to ring me back about our having a get-together, but nothing happened. So I decided to stroll along and see for myself. I didn't leave the Aero-Club until around half-past two, and I know your sleeping hours are pretty erratic anyway. So I took the chance. That Verry happened to open the door wasn't my fault. We strolled down the drive and talked."

Bruce was silent, all the old sense of suspicion and jealousy devouring him. He had never been able to forget that Jack Anderson had been his greatest rival for Verona's hand.

"That's the truth," Verona said simply. "Anything wrong with it? Or don't you trust your best friend?"

"Obviously," Bruce said, "you have still a lot to learn in regard to our conventions, Verry. Get in the house."

"But, Bruce, I was—"

"Get in!" Bruce commanded, and at that she turned reluctantly and drifted away up the drive, a dim ghost of a girl with her hair and raiment flowing. Bruce swung, looking at Anderson's dogged face in the moonlight.

"You're a damned suspicious devil, aren't you?" Anderson demanded. "I'd never have thought it of you!"

"That cuts both ways! Verona is my wife, Jack, and if you must see her make it at a decent hour next time! And I'd much prefer that there never is a next time! Good night!"

Bruce did not stay to see the effect of his words. He went back into the house, closed the door quietly, and then caught up with Verona in the bedroom. She was seated in the chair by the window, crying softly to herself.

"Now what?" Bruce demanded brutally.

"Nothing...except that I wish you didn't distrust me so! There was nothing wrong in seeing Jack!"

"That's a matter of opinion. It just so happens, Verry, that there are some things that just aren't done—and meeting an ex-lover at three in the morning on the driveway is one of them."

"I didn't ask him to come, did I?"

"I wouldn't know. He says not—but I wouldn't put anything past Jack."

Inwardly Bruce wondered why he said such a thing. He could only put it down to the insane jealousy that was consuming him. Before knowing Verona he would have trusted Jack Anderson with his life....

Then Verona got up slowly and, still weeping gently to herself, tumbled back into bed and remained there, her shoulders quivering at intervals. Bruce looked at her in the moonlight, muttered something under his breath, then returned to his own bed.

"You had the best idea of any when you said we should go back to France," he growled. "At least it will put a stop to this kind of monkey-business."

But just the same, the return to the French villa could not be accomplished immediately. There were things to be done in London first—as far as Bruce was concerned—particularly in regard to selling this city residence that he had been at pains to acquire.

"It may take a day or so to finish up my affairs in the city," Bruce said, at breakfast next morning. "Once that's done, we'll be on our way."

Verona did not reply. Pale and ghostly she sat at the other side of the table, lost in her thoughts. That brief mood of gaiety she had possessed the previous evening had utterly gone. She was again the despondent, cheerless, washed-out creature that impetuous Bruce found so difficult to understand.

"Did you hear what I said?" he asked deliberately, after a while.

"I heard. When you're ready to go, I am."

"All right. In the meantime, whilst I have to be absent, don't get up to any tricks. You don't know enough yet about our ways to be left to your own devices."

Verona gave one look, and it had such scorn in it that he felt himself writhe. He knew he must sound unnecessarily harsh, but most of it was engendered by his fear of losing her. Deep down there was nobody he loved more than Verona, and the very thought of Jack Anderson muscling in made him bristle.

It was towards ten o'clock when Bruce left the house in his sports car to make the necessary arrangements in the city for the disposal of his house. This, together with a few business calls, kept him occupied until towards noon, at which time his thoughts turned towards lunch. No use going home and driving back to the city centre, for he had still a few things to finish off.

Rather than use his car in the congested city streets he walked the distance to the Owl Café, one of his favourite haunts, but it was just as he was passing the end of one of the multitudinous side streets that he noticed something. He saw it, went a few paces, and then realised what he had seen. He went back to make sure and from a distance found himself looking at Captain Jack Anderson's enormous red sports car. It was on the point of halting at the kerb, its exhausts purring. Then it came to a stop.

Bruce watched, that old tide of suspicion sweeping back over him. He found himself becoming rigid as from the car there stepped Anderson himself, then a slim, golden girl with ebon hair. That it was Verona there was no doubt. There was no other woman quite like her.

Bruce, his eyes narrowed, waited until the pair had vanished in the doorway opposite the car, then he idled forward to investigate. The place was an exclusive restaurant, such as abound in the city centre. And Jack Anderson and Verona were together—again!

What happened to him then Bruce was not quite sure. He did not stop to reason the thing out. Instead he plunged straight across the road, through the sumptuous open doorway and into the midst of the soft-carpeted, low-lighted expanse, nearly bowling over an immaculate waiter in his cyclonic entry. There were few diners, but those who were present stared in amazement at this sudden intrusion in the opulence,

Bruce ignored them and brought up short at the table where Verona and Jack Anderson had only just seated themselves.

"Well, if it isn't Bruce!" Anderson exclaimed cordially, getting to his feet. "Quite a—"

He was going to say 'coincidence' but the next thing he knew he was crashing backwards into the next table—fortunately empty—his mouth salty with blood and his head spinning.

"Bruce!" Verona cried, horrified.

"Out you get!" he said curtly, gripping her arm fiercely. "There's going to be no more of this!"

"But Bruce, I was only—"

Bruce did not give the girl a chance to explain. He gripped even more savagely, gave a brief glance back towards Anderson as he struggled to his feet, and then bundled the girl out ahead of him through the open doorway. From the restaurant there were amazed stares.

"For heaven's sake, you madman, let me go!" Verona insisted, trying to drag free. "What in the world's come over you?"

"Common sense, if anything. Jack Anderson's playing the game a bit too freely for my liking! In you get!"

Verona struggled and protested, but against Bruce she was powerless. He bundled her into his racer, slid in beside her, and then slammed the door. In a matter of seconds his ideas of lunch forgotten, he was weaving into the midst of the city traffic and. rather to his surprise, there was no sign of Anderson's red sports car following in the rear.

"Very clever," Bruce said at length, with a bitter glance towards the silent, pale-faced girl. "The moment my back's turned off you go with Anderson again! Can't you get it through your head that you're married to me—not him!"

"Even a married woman can have men friends—and does!" Verona retorted hotly. "I've learned that much about your laws, anyhow!"

"Oh, so it's just a friendship!" Bruce sneered. "Sneaking down back streets into classy restaurants, into one where there wasn't the remotest chance of my finding you, except by coincidence—which in this case came off."

"There was no sneaking about it. Jack called not ten minutes after you'd gone this morning, and finding me all alone, he did what any decent friend would do and asked me out to dinner. If you think that was arranged, think again! He couldn't possibly have known that you'd be in town on business."

True enough, he couldn't have known—but Bruce saw no reason to admit the fact, even to himself. He was firmly obsessed with the idea that something was going on between Verona and Jack Anderson, and it had got to be stopped.

"Anyway, it won't happen again," he snapped. "We're leaving for France by the five o'clock plane and with luck we'll be at the villa by late this evening. And if Jack turns up again, I'll break his blasted neck."

Verona glanced. "You've finished all your city business, then?"

"Everything needful. Other odds and ends can wait. It's you I've got to keep my eye on!"

Verona relaxed and said no more, but there seemed to be something pretty close to tears in her eyes. Bruce noticed them when he stole an occasional look at her during driving, but he did not soften his attitude one fraction. Ruled by insane jealousy as he was, he just could not consider the situation impartially. His love for Verona was of the fiercely possessive type, which set everything else at naught.

Once they arrived home again he wasted no time in booking seats on the five o'clock plane for Southern France. That done, he had his belated lunch, then got the servants to work with the packing. All the time, through the remainder of the afternoon, he expected Jack Anderson to turn up and say his piece, but there was no sign of him. This more than ever satisfied

Bruce that Anderson was in the wrong and evidently was not going to commit himself—unless of course he intended later to bring an action for assault.

Whatever the machinations behind the scenes, Bruce kept to his original plan, and he and Verona were on the five p.m. plane—and, as he had hoped, the airport taxi brought them to their closed villa towards eight o'clock that same evening. As he unlocked the front door Bruce looked about him on the warm calm of the summer evening. For miles there was nothing but an expanse of misty emptiness terminated eventually by the line of the sea.

"Here perhaps," Bruce said, "we'll get a bit of peace! We ought never to have left it in the first place."

He held the door open, and without a word Verona went ahead of him. Once they were in the lounge, the soft lights switched on to dispel the advancing twilight, Bruce felt that Verona reminded him very much of a frightened child. Her great eyes were staring at him, and her face seemed unusually pale.

"Even if you hadn't suggested coming here I would have done," he said. "You've a lot to learn, my dear, before I dare let you out into the world again. Should be plenty of time to do it here—no servants, no neighbours. Just ourselves. See what you can do to get a meal together whilst I take the bags upstairs."

Bruce picked the bags up and turned towards the door; then a sudden thought seemed to strike him. He looked back at the girl.

"Come to think of it, just in case you decide to break

away, or on the chance that Jack Anderson might guess we're here and come after you, it might be a good idea to have the place guarded. I'll ring up the local gendarmerie and see what I can do."

"I'm your wife, Bruce, not a prisoner!" Verona declared passionately.

"That you're my wife is something that you and Jack conveniently forget! I'm going to stop that right now."

Bruce went on his way into the hall and picked up the phone. With his world-famous reputation, he had no difficulty in fixing it with the local prefect of police to have a couple of guards to watch the villa. Bruce's reasons sounded cogent enough—fear of burglary from those wanting to steal some of his valuable artefacts. Possibility of scientists trying to kidnap his wife for anthropological study— Yes, definitely. Two gendarmes would be sent immediately for night duty and two others would relieve them by day. Bruce smiled grimly to himself and went on his way up the staircase....

* * * * * * *

In half an hour the gendarmes were in position outside the villa, well concealed. When Bruce told her of their arrival, Verona made no comment. Nor indeed did she say a word throughout the remainder of the evening. It made Bruce fume inwardly to be thus treated, even though he reflected inwardly that he probably deserved it. He could not understand whether the girl was being deliberately sulky or whether she was once again reverting to that mysterious apathy which had possessed her before he had suggested she should move to city life.

In any event, the evening closed without her saying a word, and still without commenting she retired to bed. When Bruce went upstairs half an hour later he could not be sure whether she was asleep or not. Either way she did not say anything to him.

Verona was not asleep, anything but. She lay motionless until she was reasonably satisfied that Bruce had dozed off, then she very silently slid out of her own bed on the far side and quietly donned robe and slippers. Without making a sound she glided out of the room, closed the door gently, the hurried swiftly along the corridor and down the staircase.

The moment she opened the front door the shadow figures of the gendarmes loomed. They both saluted respectfully in the starlight.

"A lovely night, officers," Verona said lightly. "To lovely to sleep. It is a night for walking."

"*Oui*, madame," one of the officers agreed, but he seemed to hesitate. So Verona moved gracefully towards him.

"Can I persuade you two gentlemen to say nothing to my husband if I take a stroll?" she asked gently. "Then perhaps, afterwards, I shall be able to sleep."

Without waiting for the answer Verona began to move on her way, but to her surprise her arm was grasped and the gendarme looked down upon her seriously.

"With regret, madame," he said, in awkward English. "Your husband insisted nobody enter villa— and nobody leave. Not even you, madame!"

"What!" Verona gazed in anger. "You mean to tell me even I cannot—"

"Orders, madame. Please do not make it difficult for us."

There was more than anger in Verona's eyes now: it was very near consternation, but just the same she had the sense to realise that the gendarmes would use force if necessary. So, controlling herself as best she could, she returned to the villa and closed the front door. On re-entering the room she paused for a moment, aware of Bruce standing in his dressing gown beside the window. Though the lights were not on his silhouette was plain enough.

"Wandering around again, eh?" he asked dryly. "I'll bet you didn't get far, either!"

"Just what sort of a woman do you think I am?" Verona demanded angrily, striding across to him. "How dare you keep me a prisoner in my own home?"

"Our home, Verry. I'm as much entitled to it as you are.... I'm not keeping you a prisoner. I'm simply protecting you from the attentions of the unwanted. There's a moral code existing in our society and you're going to learn it, even if it's the hard way!"

"All I wanted to do was go for a walk in the night! What's wrong with that?"

"Of itself, nothing, only the unfortunate fact is that I don't trust you to let it end there. For all I know you may have some secret arrangement with Jack Anderson—or even some other man for all I know—and I'm not taking the risk. Until I am sure that you have the right idea about our conventions, you'll remain in this villa, and nobody will see you unless I'm present."

Verona clenched her fists. "You'll regret it, Bruce—How you'll regret it! If you won't allow me freedom to go outside, I'll—"

"Well, what?" Bruce asked coldly.

Verona did not answer. She turned away, and there was a curious droop to her shoulders. It struck Bruce transiently that her reaction to being held a virtual prisoner was more profound than he had expected, but that still did not make him yield. He was determined to jealously guard Verona, to the death if need be.

So resolute was his decision he did not attempt to go to bed again. He remained on a semi-dozing sentry duty, ready to act if the girl showed signs of trying to escape somehow—but she made no attempt to do so. She slept fitfully and awoke with the dawn, a look of utter and haggard desperation on her elfin face. It was so abject even Bruce was inwardly disturbed.

"If you must go out, if only for exercise, I'll come with you," he volunteered. "That's fair enough, isn't it?"

All he got was a faraway look, as though Verona did not even see him. It was not contempt, or hatred: it was something he could not fathom. He muttered something to himself and stalked from the room to prepare for shaving....

Since there were no servants present, Verona herself got the breakfast together, but she ate hardly anything. Most of the time throughout the meal she sat with her chin on her hand, her peculiar eyes looking through Bruce with an unnerving stare.

"Oh, for heavens' sake!" he exploded at last. "Let's go and take a walk, then maybe you'll stop sulking!"

"If anything happens to me, Bruce," Verona said in a remote kind of voice. "you'll be entirely responsible."

"Meaning what?"

"Meaning that if I am not allowed freedom to wander as I choose, I shall die. It's as simple as that. There's a biological reason why I must have freedom."

"Very unconvincing," Bruce growled. "Your people are no different to ours, except in a few physical points. That excuse won't work, Verona."

She shrugged. "Very well. Don't say I haven't warned you!"

After which she closed up into one of those utter silences of hers, and Bruce did not know what to think. He was pretty sure she was up to some kind of subterfuge, but on the other hand she did look ghostly and strange, as though she was somehow mysteriously wasting away. Just because she couldn't wander about alone? Ridiculous!

The morning, crushing in its silence, passed slowly. Bruce wandered in and out of the villa in the bright sunlight, and the day-duty gendarmes eyed him respectfully. Verona remained in the lounge, sprawled on the divan, staring into space. Since she made no effort to remove the breakfast traces, Bruce finally did it himself, his temper by no means sweet.

When it came to lunch Verona refused it—and the same thing happened again in the evening after Bruce had spent an infuriating afternoon devising something for the evening meal.

"What's the idea?" he asked bluntly. "Going on a hunger strike because I won't let you go out? It would be more to the point if you'd look after the domestic details instead of mooning the hours away on that divan!"

"Be still more to the point if you'd get the servants back," Verona responded, breaking silence at last. "The same ones we had before.... As for the hunger strike conception, it isn't that. I just cannot eat until I've taken a walk—"

"Outside and alone!" Bruce finished for her, nodding grimly. "Well you're not doing, so forget it!"

Silence. Verona relaxed again on the divan, her face deathly pale and one arm dangling limply so her fingers just touched the carpet. In spite of himself, Bruce was troubled. In one way she seemed to be ill: in another she might be capable of clever acting. No! He set his jaw. This issue had to be fought out to a finish. Verona had to realise, even by suffering if necessary, that he was the absolute master of their union.

So he ate his none-too-perfect evening meal by himself with Verona lounging nearby and completely disregarding him.... The evening was one of continued silence and, on Bruce's part, suppressed emotions. He

was thankful when the time approached for retiring—
Then, to his surprise, there came a sudden and violent
commotion from the terrace outside. There were wild
shouts in French, the crack of a gun, then swiftly
running feet.

In a matter of seconds Bruce had hurtled to the still
open French windows. To his amazement he saw one
of the gendarmes firing savagely at something across
the grounds in the twilight. The other gendarme
lay sprawled on the terrace, his throat mangled and
bleeding from some ferocious attacker.

"What the devil...?" Bruce whispered, then saw that
Verona had crept to his side and was gazing with him.
He ignored her and strode to the gendarme with the
gun.

"M'sieu!" The gendarme had only just caught sight
of Bruce and Verona. "A monster attacked—killed
Pierre. See—here are the signs."

Bruce followed the excited man quickly and presently found himself looking at a churned-up mass of
soil amidst a multitude of crushed flowers and bushes.
Though the light was fast dying, the evidence of enormous feet was there. Three-toed feet, and in propor-
tion the owner of them must have been close on eight
or nine feet high.

"Was it—a man?" Bruce asked haltingly.

"No, no, m'sieu!" The gendarme gesticulated.
"Somethink I nevaire see before! Huge! I cannot
describe it— it was grey."

Bruce frowned worriedly. The immediate thought

leapt into his mind that this monstrous unknown thing must have been trying to get at Verona and attack her. That automatically swung him around towards her to demand an explanation—but she had gone completely from the terrace

"Damn!" he yelled in fury. "My wife's gone whilst we've looking here— Where is she? Verona! *Verona*!"

He blundered back to the terrace and looked desperately about him. Then he turned back to the gendarme and snatched his gun. At the same moment there were sounds on the terrace, and Bruce immediately swung round, his weapon levelled. His feelings were definitely mixed. Coming up in the twilight was the burly form of Captain Anderson.

"Well?" Bruce spat at him. "What the hell do you want?"

"A word with you—a word that may settle your ridiculous suspicions about Verona—"

"I've no time for 'em, or for you. As for Verry, she's just run off somewhere, and if I don't find her quickly she'll be killed! Out of my way—"

"Killed?" Anderson held Bruce's arm tightly. "What are you talking about?"

Bruce explained briefly, then turned to go on again.

"Hold it a minute!" Anderson commanded, his voice dead level. "It's about this very monster that I came to talk to you."

Bruce hesitated, surprised. "The monster? But I thought you'd come to get your own back for my laying you out in that café—"

"Lord, no! You don't think I'd bother to fly from England on a matter as trifling as that, do you? Look, Bruce, there's something you've got to know about Verry—"

"I think I know it already. She's in love with you— Now get out of my way."

Anderson only tightened his grip. "Hear me out, you impetuous idiot! You take all mention of this monster far too lightly. It isn't of this country! Understand?"

"I'd gathered that, therefore it must have come from South America. How, I don't know—but it's obviously after Verry and I've got to find her—"

With that Bruce broke free of Anderson's grip and began running desperately in the dying light, searching the ground, finding traces of Verona's high heel prints, and then going on again. Anderson caught up with him in a matter of moments and helped him, but this time he made no attempt to restrain him.

"It looks," Bruce said finally, breathing hard and still holding the gendarme's gun, "as though the monster caught up with her here because this is where her footprints vanish— But the monster's go on."

He followed the unmistakable prints, visible in the sandy soil of the open land beyond the grounds of the villa, and finally paused as he came to a rising stretch of ground that was not very far from the seashore. Here, in common with most of this coast, there were numberless craters and underground entrances, probably casting back to pirate days. The light had almost gone, but what there was of the western afterglow cast upon the giant prints leading straight into one of the many surface openings.

"Thinking what I'm thinking?" Bruce demanded, as Anderson stopped beside him.

"Uh-huh—that Verry's been carried into that cave opening by the monster."

Bruce thought swiftly, then: "It's only ten minutes to the villa and back. Hop over and get my torch from the bureau. We can't investigate properly without it."

"Okay." Anderson gave a bitter smile. "Even now you don't trust me alone with Verry, do you? Even now you think I might find her and—"

"Oh, get moving, for God's sake!"

Anderson shrugged and then broke into a swift, athletic run. Bruce waited in desperate impatience, calling Verona by name meanwhile, but he got no answer from the cave's depths....

The night had completely dropped by the time Anderson came running into view again, the torch beam blazing. Instantly Bruce grabbed it from him and plunged into the cave opening, following thereafter a narrow tunnel in the dust of which were the plain imprints of a monstrous pair of feet and also, strangely enough, those of a man and woman. Bruce stared at the prints and then caught Anderson's taut smile.

"You know something about this?" Bruce demanded.

"Certainly I do. I helped Verry to bring the monster in here."

"You did what?" Bruce's brain was going round in circles. "You mean that monster is threatening her because you planned it?"

"Of course not! I—"

Bruce didn't wait for any more. He lashed out with his fist and the blow was powerful enough to knock Anderson to his knees. Bruce gave him one glance, then again shouting the girl's name he raced on down the tunnel, following prints—and all of a sudden he came upon a sight which his blood freeze.

At this point the tunnel widened into a small-sized cave and in the depths of this cave was an object similar to an octopus as far as its bladder-like body was concerned. It had an incredible number of tentacles, yet stood upon two massive three-toed feet. This was bad enough, but in the midst of tentacles there lay sprawled the body of Verona. At first she appeared to be unconscious, but after a second or two the light of Bruce's touch aroused her. Instantly she screamed, even though she could not see who was behind the glare.

"Don't shoot—!" Her cry came a split second after Bruce had fired deliberately at the loathsome monstrosity. "Don't! *Don't!*"

Bruce took no notice. He fired again, straight to the main sac of the monster. Evidently .the bullet went home, for the 'creature' quivered, dropping Verona, and then began to sag and deflate like a balloon with the air escaping. Just in time she dragged herself clear of the collapsing body and staggered over to where Bruce was standing. He caught her tightly.

"Evidently just in time," he muttered.

"You—you shouldn't have killed him," Verona whispered. "You shouldn't—you *shouldn't*!"

Bruce found her becoming a dead weight in his grasp and quite naturally assumed she had fainted from reaction. He laid her on the floor, deflecting the torch beam so the glare did not shine directly upon her.

"Shouldn't have killed him?" he repeated, astonished. "But he was all set to devour you—!"

"He wasn't—he wasn't. That's where you're so wrong. He was just about to feed me. Now—now he can never do it...."

Verona's words trailed off and she became silent. Bruce stared at her, her head pillowed on his arm, then he glanced up as he heard the slow footsteps of Captain Anderson entering the cave.

"You should have let me explain instead of knocking me down," Anderson said quietly. "Verona, in common with all her people, is a parasite. I've always known it because of my biological skill, but you didn't."

"Parasite?" Bruce mouthed the word. "How—how do you mean?"

"I mean that Verona's race have no true life of their own. They are compelled at intervals to absorb a life-fluid from a parent creature, of which there is one to each of them. No one parent can possibly feed another parasite. When you killed this one, you killed Verona too."

Bruce was deadly silent. Anderson's voice seemed to echo.

"I knew about it, but would have married Verona

had she agreed. Just as we need oxygen sometimes to save us in crisis, so Verona's people have to absorb life-fluid from their parent monster to keep them alive. One doesn't notice that in the ordinary way since it's a thing they keep themselves. That's why they remained hidden from the rest of the world—until your expedition discovered them. Verona had enough fluid in her to stay reasonably well until England was reached, and she was hoping to try and use synthetic fluid to take the place of her 'parent'. I've been in contact with scientists who are secretly working on that—but so far they've failed. She got rid of you in Scotland and enlisted my help to fly to South America and get her monster-parent. It was not difficult. I helped her get it back here. The other times Verry and I met were pure coincidence and not planned. She suggested coming back to the villa so she could be near the monster."

"So that was why she wanted to walk out alone?"

"Yes. But your damned jealous disposition wouldn't let her!"

"Why couldn't she have told me?"

"Because she was afraid of losing you. She felt you would so nauseated at the facts that you'd throw her overboard, and she loved you very dearly."

"Loved? *Loved?* Why do you say that? Why the past tense?" Bruce demanded; then without waiting for the answer, "You're lying, Jack! You rang up while I was in Scotland. If you went to South America, you couldn't have done that!"

"Hudson was well paid to play his part," Anderson

replied quietly, taking Verona's wrist.

Bruce was silent. He stared at the ashy-faced girl, then at the monster that he had slain. He could not be blamed for having assumed the creature was deadly.

"A little less jealousy, Bruce, and a little more understanding would have made your union with Verona a wonderful thing," Anderson said slowly. "As it is, she will walk no more. No other 'parent' can provide life-fluid. There is no interchange. The monster knew it was time for Verona to have the fluid, hence it came to her, since didn't come to it."

"You—you mean it knew where to look for her?"

"Certainly—with all the instinct of the homing pigeon. If she had had the fluid last night, she'd be alive and well now."

"I stopped her," Bruce whispered. "I stopped her! I was obsessed with the belief that she was having an affair."

"Jealousy," Anderson said slowly, "has brought empires in the dust. You need be jealous no more, Bruce. Verona is dead."

ABOUT THE AUTHOR

British writer JOHN RUSSELL FEARN was born near Manchester, England, in 1908. As a child he devoured the science fiction of Wells and Verne, and was a voracious reader of the Boys' Story Papers. He was also fascinated by the cinema, and first broke into print in 1931 with a series of articles in *Film Weekly.*

He then quickly sold his first novel, *The Intelligence Gigantic*, to the American magazine, *Amazing Stories.* Over the next fifteen years, writing under several pseudonyms, Fearn became one of the most prolific contributors to all of the leading US science fiction pulps, including such legendary publications as *Astounding Stories*, *Startling Stories*, *Thrilling Wonder Stories*, and *Weird Tales.*

During the late 1940s he diversified into writing novels for the UK market, and also created his famous superwoman character, The Golden Amazon, for the prestigious Canadian magazine, the Toronto *Star Weekly.* In the early 1950s in the UK, his fifty-two novels as "Vargo Statten" were bestsellers, most notably his novelization of the film, *Creature from the Black Lagoon.*

Apart from science fiction, he had equal success with westerns, romances, and detective fiction, writing an amazing total of 180 novels—most of them in a period of just ten years—before his early death in 1960. His work has been translated into nine languages, and continues to be reprinted and read worldwide.